EAST ATLANTA

ALSO BY SUSAN MINOT

Thirty Girls

Poems 4 A.M.

Rapture

Evening

Folly

Lust & Other Stories

Monkeys

Why I Don't Write

Why I Don't Write

· AND OTHER STORIES ·

Susan Minot

ALFRED A. KNOPF

NEW YORK   2020

THIS IS A BORZOI BOOK

PUBLISHED BY ALFRED A. KNOPF

Copyright © 2020 by Susan Minot

All rights reserved. Published in the United States by Alfred A. Knopf, a division of Penguin Random House LLC, New York, and distributed in Canada by Random House of Canada, a division of Penguin Random House Canada Limited, Toronto.

www.aaknopf.com

Knopf, Borzoi Books, and the colophon are registered trademarks of Penguin Random House LLC.

These stories were first published in the following places:

"Why I Don't Write" (2018) on *LitHub*, "The Torch" (1993) in *The Mississippi Review*, "Listen" (2018) in *It Occurs to Me We Are America*, "Occupied" (2017) and "Boston Common at Twilight" (2019) in *Narrative*, "Polepole" (as *"Pole, Pole,"* 2009) in *The Kenyon Review*, "While It Lasts" (1991) in *Voices Louder Than Words*, "Green Glass" (1992) in *The Atlantic Monthly*, "Café Mort" (as "Mort's Café," 2009) in *H.O.W.*

Library of Congress Cataloging-in-Publication Data
Names: Minot, Susan, author.
Title: Why I don't write : and other stories / Susan Minot.
Identifiers: LCCN 2019052531 (print) | LCCN 2019052532 (ebook) |
ISBN 9780525658245 (cloth) | ISBN 9780525658252 (ebook)
Classification: LCC PS3563.14755 (print) | LCC PS3563.14755 (ebook) |
DDC 813/.54—dc23
LC record available at https://lccn.loc.gov/2019052531
LC ebook record available at https://lccn.loc.gov/2019052532

Jacket image: lolostock/Alamy
Jacket design by John Gall

Manufactured in the United States of America
First Edition

To Jordan Pavlin
con amore

Contents

Why I Don't Write

· *POLEPOLE* ·

Goodness, she said. That was something.

You're something.

With you I am. Apparently.

She looked across the room of the cottage to heavy curtains which blocked out the daylight.

That sliver of light, she said, it's totally white. You can't see the trees or grass or anything. It must be late.

The African noon, he said.

It's blinding.

Too bright to go out in. You better stay right here.

She said, I don't even know where I am.

·

The night had ended late. It had started way back there at the engagement party she'd gone to with Bragg. Bragg was the ex-fiancé of a friend of hers in London and the bureau chief of the *Guardian* in Nairobi who'd taken her under his wing when she'd arrived in Kenya a couple of weeks ago. He seemed to know everyone at the Muthaiga Club in the crowd which spread out to a lantern-lit interior garden. At one point he called to a tall man who walked toward them, looking at her. This was one of his boys, Bragg said, fresh in from Mogadishu tonight, and Bragg had winked, leaving her to chat with the man. Then it was Bragg who had corralled them both afterward to go to dinner at the restaurant in Langata. The restaurant was called the Carnivore, and waiters sliced long strips of meat from spits sticking up on carts which were wheeled from table to table so you could choose zebra, antelope, buffalo, ostrich. The side walls of the restaurant were low with a space open to the black night. A thatched roof towered above. She and the man sat beside each other at the long table, but chatted with everyone else, shouting above the noise. At the end of the meal the man turned to her, smiling with a presumptuous look.

Connected to the eating area by a concrete ramp was a throbbing dance floor with another bar and tables and chairs. After dinner the group flowed down the ramp and disappeared into the jumbling crowd and danced and drank more beer. They danced till the crowd began to thin out.

In an unlit parking lot Bragg was sorting out rides. Some people were going back to somebody's house and there was the usual indecision and stumbling and pulling of sleeves and keys stabbing blindly at ignitions. She told the man she really did need to call it a night even though, which she didn't tell him, she wasn't working the next day, and all he said was he had a car. Coming out of the restaurant's driveway to the main road, the red taillights of the other cars turned to the left, floating one after another in the darkness. He and she, in a partly open Jeep, turned to the right.

They passed no other cars on the road, so the only light was the dim topaz bar cast by the headlights of his rattletrap Jeep. Sometimes the road was paved, with enormous black craters bitten out of it, then it would revert to rust-colored dirt, polished hard with a deep rut, like a road beside a farmer's field.

As the Jeep rounded a bend it lurched off the road. She thought he had lost control. Then he applied the brake and she saw they were in a pull-over. She looked at the man, whose face was solemn, staring ahead.

What is it? she said.

He said he needed to kiss her. He said it still looking through where the windshield was detached from the hood to the darkness beyond the headlights.

The direct statement stunned her and made her laugh. A direct statement often had that effect. She sat there, powerless. It was a welcome feeling. She felt the outline of herself begin to dissolve.

When they eventually pulled back onto the road, the Jeep made a sharp U-turn and headed back toward his place.

She rode in the passenger seat on the left side, not the right. Many things here in Kenya were like that, opposite or unexpected. This was the sort of moment she waited for, to be whisked away in the dark. It was not something you could do on your own. So much of what Daisy did was on her own. Though on your own had its advantages. On your own you could pick up and leave. You could visit new lives and try them on for a while. And what else was life for but to check it out?

She rode with a hand on the roll bar, taking the bumps as if riding waves. His kiss had both woken her up and made her sleepy. A warm air blew around them in the dark.

They turned onto a smaller road and drove till they came to a driveway. The Jeep stopped in front of a metal gate. A figure rose up out of the darkness. The face turned toward the headlights, squinting with an offended expression. He was one of many Maasai warriors who'd left a nomadic life on the savannas to work as *askaris*, guards outside houses in Nairobi's suburbs. This *askari* wore a gigantic overcoat, his black-and-red-plaid *shuka* showing below the hem. He lifted his spear in greeting, ducked away from the light, and went to unwind a heavy chain from the gatepost. He walked the swinging gate out toward the car and stood beside it as the Jeep drove in.

Does he stay out there all night? she said.

The man shrugged. He'll go back to sleep.

They drove up a short hill, rocking side to side in the ruts, then stopped in a turnaround in front of an unlit cottage. Paned French doors reflected the light back at them. At some distance to the right she could see the pale shape of a low building with one small window and a door. When the headlights went off, everything was black. She saw nothing as he led her to the door and, after turning a heavy lock, brought her inside.

•

You're right here, he said. That's where you are.

They lay in bed with the curtains closed and the noon light

slashing a blade of light across the floor. From the front room, the other room in the cottage, came the sound of something like a couch or a table being scraped across the concrete floor.

What's that? She looked alarmed.

Nothing. Just Edmond.

Who?

My man. The extent of my staff.

That's what you call him, your man?

No, I call him Edmond. Edmond takes very good care of me. He has done for a long time. He lives in that little place next door with one of his wives.

How many does he have?

Three, poor sod.

In the other room a radio went on, very loud, then immediately switched off.

He's in there tidying up. It's okay.

What's okay? she said.

·

After a while she said, Doesn't anyone around here have to work? Besides Edmond.

No.

Don't we have to get to work?

Sure, he said. Let's go to work.

Really.

No, really. I'm ready. He wrapped his arms around her.

I thought you said you had a story to file.

It would probably give Bragg a heart attack if I handed in a story on time. The man spoke with a Kenyan accent. We are not in a hurry hee-ah.

Then he said, God, what are you doing to me?

She gave a small laugh, unconvinced.

You're dangerous, he said.

Okay, she said. I was wondering if you were sincere. Now I know. You're not.

From the front room a door banged shut, rattling panes.

You're brave to be here, he said.

How's that?

Usually I scare them off.

She looked at his profile. It was not unusual for a man in his late thirties to have an unlined face, but the man's skin was unusually smooth and fair. It was not a face which would scare off a woman.

Them? she said. She looked past him to the curtains. They were thick and white but looked dark in the shadows. She sat up a little.

Hey, she said, something just went by. She narrowed her eyes. A red streak.

Where?

Out the window. In that sliver of light.

He lifted his head off the pillow, looked concerned for a moment, then lay back down. Who knows, he said.

Doesn't worry you?

Can't, he said.

You're not worried about the attacks?

Oh, them. We've always had the attacks. They're just more newsworthy to the world at large for the moment. It's nothing new for us. He closed his eyes. If you let yourself worry here, you'll go mad.

I thought everyone here *was* mad.

He opened one eye, interested. So she had been listening to what he'd said the night before. He peered back toward the sliver of light. Could be anyone out there, he said. Edmond's got nine children. At last count.

Yikes. Are they all next door?

No, but Cecily lets them visit. Not all wives do. Cecily rules the roost. She also does all my clothes washing.

Your staff is expanding.

He held his fist to her chin.

Where do the other wives live?

In Kibera.

People here are spoiled, she said.

Not in Kibera, he said.

She gave him a withering look. The whites, I mean.

Did you know Kibera is one of the largest slums in the whole world? he said. Something to make us Kenyans proud.

Yes, she said. I did know.

She looked past him into the shadowy room. There was a kilim-covered hassock near a side table with a beige dial phone on it. Clothes were gathered in small piles at the edge of the room and newspapers and books rose in loose stacks against the wall. Hanging in the doorway instead of a door was a purple-and-yellow-striped *kikoi* with dangling tassels. On the wall beside it was a large black-and-white photograph of a Maasai warrior leaping a few feet into the air above a dusty cloud. A heavy iron hatstand made by a local artist whose ironwork she'd noticed in other Nairobi houses held a dirt-spattered oilcloth coat, a few safari hats with brims, and, balanced on top, a carved wooden club called a *rungu* with its persimmon-shaped knob. She looked at the room, but she was thinking of the Kibera slum. She'd been filming the children there at an orphanage. Most of her previous work had been in nature documentaries; she'd not seen this sort of poverty up close before. At first the children she was filming had watched her with an expectant stare as if she were about to burst into flame. Then gradually they became animated till they were swirling around her like a school of fish, showing perplexingly joyful smiles. These children had lost their parents mostly to disease and were living in a place made up of a jumble of lean-tos the size of armchairs and she couldn't get over how much they smiled. The camera around her neck cost more than most of them would see in a lifetime. Many of the children were infected with the disease. She told herself, I am here to help, a weak plea of self-justification against the shame she felt seeing her life in comparison to theirs. She had an even more uneasy feeling she admitted to no one, that in some way she was worse off.

We are spoiled, said the man with his hands crossed behind his head. But there's justice. We are also miserable wrecks. What are you looking at?

You.

The man's face may have looked untouched, but his eyes did not look spoiled. They looked worn out.

She turned onto her back and faced the ceiling. The ceiling was painted dark blue and where it met the white stucco walls you could see in the undulating line the brushstroke of a human hand. The plaster had been smoothed by hand, too, giving the surface a soft uneven look.

So what are you doing here? he said.

She glanced at him, not sure what he meant. His expression was relaxed.

The documentary, you know, we're—

He shook his head. I mean, really. Here, on the other side of the world.

I always wanted to come here.

His eyebrows rose.

You mean, what am I running away from? She went on in a flat tone, Nothing. Getting as far away as possible from Darien, Connecticut?

Is that where you're from?

Was.

Not anymore?

It's not a place I ever really related to, she said.

So you've come to Africa to relate?

Oh no, she said. Are you going to be one of those people?

What?

Who give you a hard time for being in Africa.

He shrugged. I just don't have a lot of patience for the thrill-seeking tourist.

She said nothing. She thought of Babette, the German woman who ran the orphanage they were filming. She was not a thrill seeker. She was a good human being with a strong center of gravity, stern one moment, loving the next. She had a purposeful manner. The first day filming Daisy had taken one look at Babette with her steady eyes and pronounced jaw and thought, Now there's the sort of person I'll never be.

•

After a while he said, I'm glad you're in Africa.

Can I ask you something? she said.

Anything. He sounded relieved.

You don't happen to have . . . Her voice trailed off and she sort of laughed. A girlfriend or a wife, do you?

Well, yes, he said in the same gentle tone. I do.

You do?

Yes I thought you knew.

Her body went still. They were both facing the ceiling and neither turned.

I thought Bragg would have told you, he said.

She shook her head. No, she said. Bragg didn't tell me.

They were silent for a moment.

Which? she said.

Which what? he said. He too seemed surprised.

Wife or girlfriend?

Wife.

They were silent again.

Children? she whispered.

Uh-huh. He cleared his throat. Two. Girls.

She turned on her side to face him, propping herself up on an elbow. She thumped him on the chest. It hit harder than she meant it to.

Ow, he said.

Sorry. She flopped onto her stomach and smushed her face into a pillow. She reached back for the tangled sheet and pulled it up over her backside. The sheets were sort of olive brown, typical bachelor sheets, she had thought.

That's okay, he said.

I'm an idiot, she said into the olive-brown pillow.

No, you're not.

I thought you lived here. One finger tapped the mattress near her ear while the rest of her remained frozen.

I do. When I'm working in Nairobi.

She peeked out one eye. How old are they?

Fiona's six and Emma's three.

Jesus. She sat up, holding the sheet around her. I didn't ask, she murmured. She looked at him. He looked back. Okay, she said, so I didn't ask.

Where are you going? he said.

Getting up. She dragged the sheet with her and stood on the thin pale rug. She scanned the dim floor for her clothes.

I thought you knew, he said.

It looked like such a bachelor pad, she said under her breath. She located her bra and wisp of a shirt. I thought . . . I mean, I wasn't even . . . I mean, whatever. I didn't want to think. She found her skirt crumpled under the bed.

Are you upset? he said.

She was putting on her clothes and stopped for a moment. I don't know, she said. Then she started moving again.

He got up. He put on fresh clothes, different from the ones he'd worn last night. He buttoned a light blue shirt, looking at each button. He went to the window and pulled back one of the curtains. More light came into the room: the gap showed a short strip of lawn and a sparse tangled wall of trees.

Where are they?

He looked over, worried.

Your family.

In Naivasha, at the lake. His voice was still gentle, but the honey had gone out of it. We have a house there.

Oh, they're out there, she said. She sounded as if she were daydreaming.

My wife grows flowers.

She looked at him, frowning.

No, he said, on a farm. It's our business, a flower farm.

Oh. That sounds nice. She found her sandals.

He continued looking out the window. My wife's really the one who runs it.

Uh-huh. She sat on the kilim-covered hassock and began strapping on her sandals. They were well-worn sandals with a wedge. She thought of how she'd gone a lot of different places in those sandals.

He looked back at her. We're apart a lot, he said.

She regarded him with lowered brows.

·

Will I see you again? he said, standing in the panel of light from the window.

Her hands were occupied with the buckling of her sandals. She didn't roll her eyes when she looked at him, but her expression was the same.

No? he said.

She rethreaded her sandal straps, first making them tighter, then making them looser. What for?

I don't know about you, he said. But that doesn't happen all the time. He pointed to the bed.

Oh, I think actually it does. She laughed.

He stepped toward her and stood there with his bare feet and light blue shirttails untucked. You said so yourself it was something.

She released her sandal and set her feet on the floor. Her mouth made a small puffy sound which seemed to deflate her. I don't know, she said. Her shoulders slumped.

I do, he said. He sat down beside her on the hassock. He slumped, too, but his shoulders were still above her head.

It was great, he whispered.

For you, she shot back, but her heart wasn't in it. Inside, she felt a flutter of panic.

He was sitting very close and she would only have had to move her head a few inches to slump against him. But she didn't. She remained in the freeze position.

She'd once worked on a documentary about the wild dogs of the Kalahari Desert. The animal behaviorist they'd interviewed was a freckled woman who in her forest-green pup tent had recited in a clipped confident lisp how prey employed one of, or some combination of, three strategies for survival: freeze, flight, or fight. The woman had added that this applied to humans as well, though that had been cut from the film.

I'm not going to say I don't love her, he said.

God, no, she murmured. She immediately added, Sorry.

She felt how near he was. She thought, I'll just stay here one more minute, then I'll stand up and smile and walk out. He'd accept that. Standing up she could still keep a small amount of her dignity intact, maybe. She would pick up her handbag and go into the front room, find her cigarettes on the driftwood tree-stump table, get a drink of water in the bare kitchenette, and wait for him to follow with the car keys. They would get back in the Jeep and he'd drive her to the guesthouse in Karen where she was staying and where she'd stay another two weeks till they finished shooting. Then she'd check out doing that story about the cattle vaccinations in Sudan and go there, or would find another story to do or another project somewhere or anything as long as it was somewhere else and Nairobi was not in it.

Daisy, he said.

What? she said, impatient.

Daisy.

She wished he wouldn't do that, say her name. She glanced up and made the mistake of looking into his face. Oh God, she thought, or didn't think. His face was full of concern. She found herself believing it. Just for a second, she said to herself and down her head came and collapsed on his chest.

•

The night before it had seemed as if she were sailing toward something warm and enveloping. Now she was being swept in a different direction. At least she was moving, she thought, in one direction or another.

•

Okay, though, now was the moment to stand up.

She didn't move and the moment passed. Another moment passed. She was still not standing.

•

Lulled by the heartbeat in her ear, she wondered if this was the moment she would look back on and think, I could have walked away, but did not.

In the quiet they both heard something crack like two sticks hitting. It came from around in front of the cottage.

Now what? he said. His head tipped forward. They heard shouts. Christ, he said. He sprang up, though his expression was not alarmed, just focused. He headed for the doorway, pulled aside the purple-and-yellow *kikoi*, and disappeared. The soles of his feet were the last thing she saw.

She heard him rattle open the front door and yell something in Swahili. The voice grew faint when he stepped outside and moved away from the house.

She stayed sitting on the hassock. After a while she heard talking, people coming back into the cottage. She heard the man. A voice answered in English with a native accent. She got up and ducked past the *kikoi* into a small hallway. She peeked out from the doorframe to see into the front room.

The man's back was to her, his hands shoved in his front pockets. A thin man stood in front of him, gesturing as he talked.

He had a dark shaved head and was wearing a cream-colored shirt with short sleeves and four pockets. That would be Edmond. He was about the same age as the man. Next to him were two boys, not quite teenagers, looking caught. The taller one wore a large red T-shirt which came almost to his knees. He didn't look at Edmond or at the man. The younger one had a dark T-shirt which said VOTE THE MIAMI WAY. His face was also tipped down, but he was watching Edmond out of the corner of his eye.

As Edmond talked, the man nodded. He shook his head. He ran his hand over his hair. At one point he lifted his arms, as if to say, Now what? Wait, Daisy thought, what had she been thinking of just now? She'd lost the thread of something . . . Oh, that's right, a wife. There was a wife. She looked at the man's back. He looked different to her now with a wife.

Edmond cleared his throat. He glanced off for a moment, as if not wanting to get to this part of the story, and saw Daisy hiding by the door. His gaze slid smoothly by her, betraying nothing of what he'd seen.

The man's hands were now clasped on top of his head. Edmond looked once at the boys, then away from them and finished what he had to say.

Everyone stood there, silent.

The man dropped his arms. He turned a stony profile to the boys. The younger one was rolling his shirt around his fist. The man spoke to the older one in the red T-shirt, asking him a question. The boy raised his eyes, blinked slowly, and said something she couldn't make out but his tone was defiant.

The man snapped. His loud voice startled Daisy in her little hall. The boy did not look startled in the least. He listened, unimpressed. When the man finished yelling the boy spat on the floor near the man's feet.

Daisy watched the man's long arm swing back and come forward and smack the boy's small face on one cheek, then with the back of his hand he smacked the other. The boy's head jerked a little with each blow, but his body didn't move. Edmond and the other boy continued to stand there. After a moment the boy in the red T-shirt raised his hand and covered his cheek. Daisy thought she saw a smile hidden by his fingers.

•

The man turned abruptly with a gesture that said, This is all nonsense and I'm not going to bother myself any further. He turned back to Edmond. He pointed out to the turnaround, and gave him some orders. Edmond nodded, though Daisy could see his attention was being pulled toward the boys, either to check if they were okay, or to continue the punishment. Daisy ducked away from the door before the man saw her.

Her heart was pounding. She went over to the window and the parted curtain. She looked out at the backyard. The brittle grass was covered with a film of dust, and at the edge of the lawn were olive bushes and thorny dwarf trees and floppy banana leaves. Half hidden by the brush was a high chain-link fence with loops of new silver barbed wire on top. Beyond the fence was a brown forest floor with spindly tree trunks and a carpet of huge maroon leaves.

•

The man came back into the room, shaking his head with tiny shakes. Sorry about that, he said.

Daisy remained at the window. He stood close behind her and parted the curtains wider and they both looked out.

What was that all about? she said. I heard you shouting.

He took a deep breath and exhaled. She felt his breath on the hair on top of her head. He put his arms loosely around her. Just the usual nonsense, he said. It was not worth going into.

She thought of the slap and shivered. Maybe he really thought it was nonsense and usual. Maybe that wasn't a lie. His arms tightened around her.

But you're still here, he said. I'm glad.

I should be going . . . Her voice trailed off.

She kept staring out at the garden. Nothing was moving in the bleached yard. She was mesmerized, trying not to think of what was behind her. She thought of the boy in the red T-shirt and his strange smile. She stared out to the garden, feeling as if *she* had been slapped. The eerie thing was it seemed as if she were right where she belonged.

·

I saw you hit that boy, she said.

The man spoke in the same calm voice. He had it coming to him, he said.

That's a little harsh, isn't it? she said.

You have to be from here to understand.

People say that a lot.

Maybe because it's true.

She heard his attention straying and turned her head. He was looking toward the other end of the lawn where a woman was hanging laundry.

Come, he said. He unclicked the lock on the tall windows. Meet Cecily.

The air was thick and warm. Daisy followed him outside as if she were in a net, still in the physical lure of him.

The woman at the clothesline wore a crimson short-sleeved dress and a printed green scarf knotted around her head. She was not tall, and when she reached to drape the clothes over a thin rope clothesline, her orange heels lifted out of flip-flops as thin as pancakes. Her figure was sturdy, her neck and arms thin. The man called to her.

Hello, Mistah T, she said, not turning. She clipped on clothespins made of pink plastic.

Cecily, I'd like you to meet my friend Daisy.

Karibu, Cecily said, and paused for a moment to tip her turbaned head in Daisy's direction. Then she bent down for more clothes.

Asante sana, Daisy said. This about exhausted her Swahili. Welcome. Thank you so much.

Daisy's from America, the man said.

Cecily nodded. She snapped open a towel, not looking up.

Since she'd been in Kenya, Daisy had noticed that she was either being stared at as a curiosity or else pointedly ignored. Occasionally she would receive a look from a stranger of direct hatred.

The man walked over to the other side of the woven yellow plastic basket and spoke to Cecily in Swahili. Being in a place where she didn't know the language, Daisy had learned to watch people instead. Often that told her enough.

Cecily listened to the man. She stared at the towel in her hand, then flung it absently up on the line. She folded her smooth arms, took a deep breath, and tucked in her chin. She looked at the man as if sizing him up. For a moment Daisy thought she was going to upbraid the man, and it filled her with an odd sort of hope.

The man mimed how he had hit the boy. Cecily nodded slowly. Yes, yes, she knew. The man shrugged and winced. Cecily shook her head in agreement. She pursed her lips. Before speaking she frowned and when she finally did say something it sounded decisive. Daisy was transfixed. Cecily was giving the man a piece of her mind. He stood listening to her now.

Then Cecily's face burst into a smile. She let her arms drop and slapped at the man's shoulder. They both laughed. Cecily kept shaking her head and the man was nodding and they laughed together at her joke. Daisy backed away from them, feeling suddenly transparent like a flame in sunlight.

•

Daisy stood waiting next to the Jeep in the driveway. Through the front window of the cottage she could see the man on the telephone with his back to her, facing the wall. Talking to the wife, she figured. It was bright outside and she was without sunglasses. She strolled off to be out of sight of the man, scuffing the ground. Many footprints had distressed the dirt. Suddenly she felt exhausted. For a moment she was back in the bed with the man. He was holding her wrist. She felt swept up again and it ran through her body. Sex was like that, not all of you came back right away. Part of you lingered with the person, not unhappily; it was nice to be relieved of yourself, though eventually that part would return.

She had moved into the shade near Edmond's house. The one door was open to a turquoise-painted wall. There was thin grass in the front yard and a small circle of charred wood. Against the ocher wash of the house sat two white molded plastic chairs. A small child appeared in the doorway, wearing a pink sleeveless dress with ruffles at the shoulders and eating a papaya. She eyed Daisy. Daisy smiled and said, *Habari.* The girl's eyes widened and she looked behind her for instruction, then stared again at Daisy.

Cecily appeared behind the little girl, carrying something, shooing her out of the door. Her arms were straining under the weight of the large gray tub. The little girl sat on a log near the burned area biting the papaya, still watching Daisy. Cecily hauled the tub to the end of the yard near some scarlet hibiscus and tossed the water out. It floated in the air like a mirror, then came down flat and made a circle of puff in the dirt.

Cecily turned around and looked at her, a white woman standing on the tan drive in her tan skirt. Daisy waved and smiled and started to step back. She rocked on her sandals. Cecily came forward a few steps and stopped. Her smooth solid face was not smiling. At first Daisy thought she was getting some version of the cold stare, the look of disapproval any girl might get stumbling out of the man's cottage, possibly one in a series of aimless white girls. But when Cecily lifted her hand to shield her eyes from the sun, Daisy saw a different expression. She was looking at Daisy with pity.

•

The man was locking the front door. Everyone here was always jangling keys. When she got into the Jeep she noticed a spiderweb of cracked glass at the center of the windshield. She hadn't seen it the night before, but it had been dark and she hadn't been looking.

The man got in the driver's seat. He turned the key a few times before the engine started. Where to? he said, and pulled at the steering wheel with an effort.

She didn't answer. It wasn't really a question. He knew where she was staying. Back where I belong, she thought. The Jeep bounced forward. They drove out the gate, which was wide open now in the daytime. Now she saw the road they'd come on. It looked as if it had been heaped with fresh dirt and raked.

Everything okay? he said.

Fine, she said. She didn't look at him. She wanted to start right then not looking at him. The sooner the better. Immediately she felt expanded. She thought, I don't even need to tell him. She couldn't remember the last time she'd felt that way, not needing to explain herself—to him, to anyone.

There was a phrase Daisy had heard a number of times in Kenya: *polepole*. It had a number of related meanings. It could mean Easy does it, one step at a time, take it slow. When it was only *pole*, it meant too bad, or that's a shame, or sorry.

It was the thing people might say to comfort someone with a little hardship. You'd say it to a child who'd scraped her knee, or to someone whose car had broken down. *Pole*. Poor you. Shame.

That had been Cecily's expression, *pole*. You poor thing. It was the understanding expression of a mother, though Daisy could not remember ever having seen the expression on her mother's face. Cecily had emphasized the look by nodding, as in, Don't forget this conversation we've had. Poor you. Shame. Step-by-step. Gentle now. How that could all be in a look, Daisy didn't know, but there it was.

When offerings like that come your way, you should take them. Bouncing in her seat, Daisy thought if she could keep Cecily's message in mind, she'd be better off. Concentrating was sometimes like praying. You had to repeat it. Careful with yourself. Gentle. The light coming through the trees threw barred shadows on the red ground. She rode through the stripes.

· THE TORCH ·

She lay back on the clean white pillows.

Is that—? Who's there? she said.

It's me.

John? she said in a weak voice. Is that you, John? Happiness came into her tone.

Yes, it's me, said her husband, taking her hand.

Where have you been?

I've been right here. You just woke up.

Are we at home?

Yes, he said. We're at the house.

You came from—? she whispered. She shook her head. No, she said. That's not . . .

Is there anything I can get you, dear?

No, John.

Here, have a little water. He held up a paper cup. His hand was shaky. He managed to guide the bent straw to her lips.

Thank you, John, she said. Saying his name pleased her. She smiled, though her husband would have hardly called it a smile.

Her face had lost most of its flesh and her profile was more pronounced, even regal.

She spoke with great effort. I'm thinking of the dancing, she
said. Isn't it lovely to think of? Her eyelids were low and her black
eyes looked elsewhere.

It is, he said. He stroked her hand. Her hand had not changed
so much, though her wedding band was loose beneath her
knuckle. But her wrist was different, flat like a board, and her fore-
arm where it emerged from her dressing gown was like a plank.

Have you changed the music, John?

What, dear?

I'm sorry, she said. I'm confused.

Painkillers, he said. The medicine is making you confused.

Her gaze flicked in his direction with a sharp bird-look, test-
ing the soundness of this. The medicine, she said uncertainly, and
nodded. What time is it?

He consulted his watch and after some time reported, Twenty
to five.

In the evening, she said with suspicion.

In the evening.

They sat for a while.

Then she said, Tomorrow I think we might go to the shore.

We'll see.

She lifted up her narrow arms and dropped them on the bedspread. Oh, God, she groaned, I'd love to swim. In lovely cold
water.

You would like that, he said.

I wanted to swim with you, John. She frowned. But they
served dinner so early.

It's all right, he said.

They kept the tables apart, but everyone danced after, she said. I thought—but then she came the next day. Her mouth turned down. What did you say to her, John?

The man shook his head.

What? she said.

I can't remember, the man said with resignation.

She was prettier than I. That, everyone knew.

I don't know about that, he said.

Couldn't dance as well though. But she was chic. I remember she had a really good-looking scarf and a wonderful suit. Better clothes than mine.

The woman's hand waved slowly; it didn't matter so much now.

You were a wonderful dancer, he said. You are.

Did you love her, John?

No, he said. I loved you.

The woman nodded, her expression placid, skin stretched over her cheekbones.

I know, she said, meaning to reassure him. I know. Her eyes closed, winglike. I wondered if you believed in Christ, she said.

Her husband watched her fall asleep. In their lifetime he'd watched her face go through many changes, but he could still see the first face he'd known when she walked up from the beach that day.

Where are we again? Her eyes stayed closed.

Home, in the house on Chestnut Street.

Oh yes. In my room.

In your room.

That's right. Her eyes opened. You'll stay here, John? You won't go away?

I won't go away.

He sat and watched her sleep, looking at her dry lips and polished forehead. Past the bed out the window, it was turning blue and he looked at his watch. The doctor was coming by after five. He stayed in the chair. He looked at his thumbs meeting each other.

After an uncertain amount of time there was a tap on the door. The doctor's head appeared, the door was pushed farther ajar. Sleeping? the doctor said.

The man nodded.

Could I talk to you? the doctor said, with a twitch of his head.

They stood side by side at the upstairs railing, both looking down at the top of the lamp on the hall table below. I want to ask, said the doctor, how you are holding up.

The man stared ahead of him, not wanting to speak.

Andrew, said the doctor. It can be hard on a man.

At the mention of his name, Andrew turned to face the doctor. Yes, he said. He knew.

· OCCUPIED ·

Riding back from her studio, Ivy thought, I'll stop for just a minute.

Already they had been here a month and she'd not gone. The sitter had to leave at five-thirty, there was supper to make, but it was pathetic she'd not checked out what was being broadcast all over the world. At an earlier time in her life she would likely have been sitting there herself—righteous, smoking cigarettes, stubborn.

She located a parking sign, propped her bike wheel with her boot, and wound the chain around the signpost. She fiddled with the padlock key till the shackle clicked in.

She stood. Wind barreled down the surrounding skyscrapers. They seemed to tilt in over the small patch of park with its rows of small trees and pig-colored polished marble descending in slabs. Across the street a low canopy of orange trees fluttered over a bank of lumpy sleeping bags and blankets looking like compressed trash, draped with a blue plastic tarp. The park set in this square looked crisp and new, smaller than she'd pictured, and less ramshackle.

Hair blew across her face. She felt for her hair elastic, but it had fallen out. That was annoying. She always kept her hair tied back. She stuffed the loose strands into her jacket collar and crossed the street to walk down the perimeter. The images she'd seen in the paper and on the screen were decidedly more monumental than what appeared before her. But wasn't it always like that? In front of you, things turned smaller, and seemingly less substantial than in a photograph, despite the fact that the real thing was actually more substantial, being three-dimensional and more complex. In front of you it was actually real. And what was more compelling than real? Images of real, apparently. To a visual artist like Ivy, this was hardly a new revelation.

She strode down the tilting concrete, as usual alone. For some time now when she was walking, it was either alone, or with her son. It was one or the other. Walking with Nicky she was continually amazed at the unquestioning faith of the little fellow, holding her hand and wholly accepting that this was where he was meant to be, beside her. He was eight, so one would think she'd have grown accustomed to it by now.

Plywood barricades rose up at the end of the block, hiding the perpetual crater of construction. Rebuilding was still going on after, what was it now, ten years? One couldn't visit the neighborhood without thinking of that day. If you'd been in New York, you had your story. Hers: out in the morning exercising, the crisp sunlight, a blue September sky smooth as church glass, and the strangest sight of the high pale tower with a plume of white smoke furling out of a black hole torn at the top. How could an airplane have been that out of control? And then the mounting awareness, as fire trucks sirened southward and shopkeepers stood with crossed arms outside their doors, that this was not an accident. Then someone at a bus stop—everyone stood staring—saying a plane had hit the Pentagon, and on the strangely trafficless Lafayette Street, dark figures hurried away from the mayhem. Men in dark suits with briefcases and women in skirts walked rapidly uptown, manic, stiff kneed. When they passed by, she saw their backs, from their heads down to their legs was powdered white. Later, drifting to Washington Square she stood among milling people facing down West Broadway to one of the towers now engulfed in white smoke. Strangers muttered to one another, astonished, How many people did the building hold? How many floors were—? when, in an instant, the tower in front of them dropped like a soufflé, vanishing before their eyes. A moan rose from the crowd. People stood frozen, then turned, they looked away, they looked back, they didn't move.

The park sidewalk where she walked now was empty, the uninteresting outside of the encampment. Across the street along the base of skyscrapers, busy working people scurried up and down the hill, entering mammoth entryways, carrying briefcases, their shopping bags twisting in the October wind.

The vision had been very like a hallucination. You could not believe what you were seeing. That was the phrase everyone kept using, they couldn't believe what they had seen. Her brain immediately registered the otherworldliness of the seconds. The image entered and she was aware in that instant that it would never leave her. Out of the thousands of images which the city gathered and posted and printed and beamed after that morning, none she saw had been from the precise place where she stood watching, as her knees buckled, dropping as the building dropped. That was one time when what was in front of her was greater in intensity than what she saw depicted after. Not like the park in front of her now, more puny than its pictures.

On that Tuesday morning, she felt that as a witness, she was a kind of custodian of the deaths. It sounded self-aggrandizing, so she never admitted the feeling, but she had taken it inside her, the obligation. But, really, what kind of custodian could one be of such a thing and what could one do with it?

The sun was no longer visible, having dropped behind the buildings, though the sky would be light for another hour. She wondered now, as she paced down the sidewalk slope, how many people had actually witnessed it, the murder of thousands of people, and how many others kept that vision inside them and felt, as she did, to be a guardian of it.

•

It looked like a statue, then she saw it was a man, dressed in a black cloak with a Darth Vader helmet, standing unmoving on a pink-and-beige polished marble platform. Around his neck a sign: I AM ONE OF THE 99%.

She continued along the outside as if unsure how much she was ready to engage. The wind funneling down the buildings hit the sidewalk and crashed like a waterfall, spinning all the thin yellow and orange leaves in its turbulence.

If he were here, she thought, he'd be here.

She felt a small triumph that she had not thought of him for—how long was it? Well, a little while at least. But now the thought of him was back, for her to ruminate over. Was he even in town? She couldn't be sure. He was more likely away, usually being somewhere else, never staying in touch, at least not with her. It had been three weeks since . . . Jesus, she thought, that person must be freezing.

She'd reached the bottom of the park where, in an open half shell area, a shirtless man was dancing, his hands miming a giant braid. A drum beat dully; a tambourine bumped a hip, and two women twirled with meaningful smiles. They held ribbons swirling, a sort of May Day dance crossed with a rumba. A sign propped on the nearby wall read: MAKE MUSIC NOT MONEY.

The movement had been both criticized and praised for its lack of definition. No leader, no clear agenda, yet it managed to convey a strong forthright expression of dissatisfaction if not fury with economic inequality in the country.

She swerved away from the circling arms of a woman in a pom-pom vest and entered the park. Between the planted areas where trees shook, along marble borders, the paths were choked with boxes and bundles, tied down like ship cargo. Plastic tarps were everywhere, some spread out, some curled like wrapping paper, some sloppily folded. It had been rainy the last few days and they must have had to cover up a lot to keep things dry. She skirted a canvas lean-to and inside saw a girl with dreadlocks, her arms looped around a bearded dog with a red bandanna. Beside them a young man wearing a bumpy oatmeal fleece and shorts above pink knees was crouched over, sewing what looked like a pouch.

Yellow police tape draped over box shrubs. She walked by an unshaven gray-haired man in a lumberjack coat sitting on a wire crate and stirring—was it soup?—in a small pot over a blue-flamed Bunsen burner. He gazed through her passing figure, as if admiring a distant valley. He could have been anywhere.

She studied the faces as she moved by. Here were the people who had managed to suspend their lives so that they could express their disapproval of the unjust ways of the world. In the faces, she saw the purposeful expression of people convinced of their reason for being here, and of their importance. The look said, I have a cause, I have conviction, I am entertaining no doubts.

A plump woman with a pink sweater falling off a creamy shoulder had a slightly startled expression—or maybe it was the high arch in her penciled eyebrows—as if ready for action, accustomed to being disturbed, and prepared for it. Her eyes darted around looking for someone. Two young men sat side by side on a tilted blanket. One had a baseball cap worn low to shield his eyes; the other was selecting chewing tobacco from a pouch and tucking it into his lower lip.

She nearly knocked over a hand-painted poster wedged between plastic bags: THE PEOPLE STAND WITH MOTHER EARTH AND NOW IT IS "SPRING" ALL OVER THE WORLD. Represented, too, were the stubborn (THIS IS SO NOT OVER), the worried (WHAT WOULD JESUS SAY?), and the wounded: a sideburned man in a battered parka had his sign: FIRED FOR NOT BEING RICH ENOUGH.

Off the path, among cloudy plastic containers with blurry contents inside, a young woman sat perched on a stool, being interviewed, her dark hair somehow solid and shaking, her skin spotted with blemishes. A man who did not look American—

crisp shirt, stylish coat, arranged red scarf, the facial structure of a greyhound—held a microphone near her dark purple mouth, while his cameraman in a Greek captain's hat shouldered a camera inches from her face. Ivy heard the soft voice—"People just don't want to see that"—before a gust blew her words off and away.

A fellow in black retro glasses was typing on a computer which rested on a large cardboard box—from a washing machine?—decorated all over with black *X*s and one large *O*, presumably for "Occupy," with a smiley face inside. A sign nearby said ENOUGH IS ENOUGH. That, she thought, admiring its wide net, could be applied to everything.

•

In her brain there was always a someone. For years it had been Nicky's dad. Since their split—more than two years ago—the place where he'd been was a ripped hole. She felt her son standing beside the black hole, baffled. She did her best to distract him, as if vigilance and concern could keep him from noticing that his father was no longer there.

(This vigilance took all her energy and attention.)

Then in had crashed Dexter Fleming. He intended in no way to make a crash, he had just appeared, interested. As far as he was concerned she was just another girl who, when he gestured with his hand to come a little closer to him on the couch, sidled obediently over to his firm round shoulder where the surprise of him being close turned out to be so massive Ivy could barely breathe. He had no intention of making the impression he did; he had no intention at all.

Enough is enough with Dexter Fleming? No, not yet. She'd not had enough. At one point she would. She could see that. There was no way it would not end, but it was not yet. She had not had enough of him yet.

She wove through the maze of bundles and plastic bags, the occasional chair, child sized, a fluttering line of Tibetan prayer flags. But he would probably have been here already, filing a report with his particular angle. People wanted to hear from Dexter Fleming, the photographer who'd been kidnapped in Iraq and escaped after three years. That he was handsome was no doubt a part of his fame, that he escaped by having a woman fall in love with him was another. It was easy to picture him here, weaving among the protesters, small potatoes compared to what he'd seen, sitting on their bundles. She thought of his perspective and tried it on. It felt like a higher, more relevant one than hers. What would he have made of it here?

•

Wait, what did she make of it? The movement seemed slightly disorganized and vague but at least they were trying, she thought. At least they were showing they cared.

•

What had she done all day? Hovered over a piece of paper, like a hawk searching the shallows far below for the shadow of a fish . . . and yet the people just sitting here . . . what was it that they were doing?

When people were united in a cause it showed on their faces. The expressions on people in a protest march were always impressive: purposeful, unapologetic, convinced. The people here however had the air of tourists on vacation, or of travelers waiting for a bus. She was catching them in a lull, but they seemed ironically unengaged—none looked up as she walked by, only inches away. They smoked cigarettes, picked at pieces of sandwiches in tinfoil. One girl lay sleeping with her mouth open, unguarded and trusting. Her presence was her offering.

A blast of wind funneled down from above, spilling leaves like confetti. Her hair scribbled over her face, blinding her. Tucking it back into her canvas collar, she flashed on his fist gripping the rope of her hair. Thank goodness people couldn't see the lurid visions in one's head. She replayed the vision, savoring the depraved thrill.

Then, as if to balance herself, she thought of Nicky, who must stay always in her sights, possibly at the moment now playing on the thick living room rug, having disassembled his igloo of toys, intent on a train, or a tractor. When she played with him, he wanted her to push the ambulance and also make the sound and also describe again the person she was rescuing . . . No, you said that he broke his arm, Mama, do that part again, you forgot the person coming out of the store, you forgot the dog, etc. The scenarios had to be repeated exactly. She was a robotic performer. She, the same person whose brain went white with light as her pants were peeled off, pushed against the wall inside the man's door, still in her winter coat . . .

She saw an area of tinfoil-covered containers, presumably where people were fed cafeteria-style. Much had been written about the fluid mode of organization. People had managed to band together. Again she wondered what the man would think of it, then again stopped herself, aware now that fathoming the man's thoughts led her swiftly down a cul-de-sac to his indifference, obtuseness, and lack of love. She pictured instead the man's room where he'd first kissed her, first took her to bed. In the day it was white with black accents; in the night it was black with white and in both rooms there was allure and radiance.

A sign propped on crimson chrysanthemums had the cutout letters of a ransom note: I AM HERE BECAUSE I AM SCARED FOR MY COUNTRY. Beside it, another: SEX WORKERS AGAINST CAPITALISM. She looked with interest for the custodians of this second sign but saw no one who matched, only a man in a Lapland hat with the flaps over his ears, fiddling with a loose button on his shirt. Other signs within sight: FUCK GOOGLE. GREED IS AN ADDICTION. REVOLT. EAT THE RICH.

She noted a theme: anger.

Initially he'd been an interesting conversation for the girls. She had to tell someone about it. This blaze. Wow, they said at lunch, shiny eyed, Fun. Good for you. Then, as he became less forthright in his intentions, or more forthright in his lack of intentions, the girls, stalwart, married, squared away themselves in that department, lost their patience on Ivy's behalf. He didn't answer texts? Not acceptable. This guy should be howling at your door, they said. Even she wasn't convinced by that. But something in her appreciated their protective rage.

After lunch everyone would gather up their pocketbooks, put on their new coats, suddenly urgent, each with her own errands, each with her own worry. They shared some troubles; some they hid. Then they all would hurry off, busy. But, no, they now said, shaking their heads with tight certainty. You don't want that. Outside under the red restaurant awning, kissing one another goodbye, they touched one another's sleeves tenderly, looked in each other's eyes. They looked down and complimented someone's new boots, then dispersed in four different directions. *You don't want that.*

But she did. She did want it.

When she lay alongside the man her body dissolved into his. And after she left the cool and hot hours in his arms, she would stay in a hypnotic state, zombielike. It was so—

Her knee knocked something to the ground. A book. She picked it up. A woman in a plaid coat glanced over her shoulder, irritated, briskly thwonking books into plastic crates which surrounded her as if she were a child playing house. Labels were marked: POLITICS. PHILOSOPHY. NOVELS. WOMEN'S STUDIES. Would there ever be a box that said MEN'S STUDIES?

Sorry, Ivy said and handed over the book. One was always so quick to apologize. Sorry! Don't mind me. Always the first reaction. The people here, their signs wedged with water jugs against the wind, leaning on plastic tarps, weren't apologizing. When you were a protester you could drop the apologetic pose, marching elbow to elbow. Twenty years ago she'd been like they were, knocking on frozen doors in the suburbs of Boston, interrupting people during warm yellow dinners with televisions colorfully swimming behind them, asking for money to protest the slaughter of Alaskan seals. She had righteous belief in the cause. Save the whales. Even then, though, she would begin with an apology: Sorry to bother you, but we are trying to stop the killing . . .

The book she had handed over was a popular novel everyone had loved. Everyone, it seemed, but she. No, no, it gets better, people said. You should keep with it. She had abandoned it early on. Why did people want you to read a book you didn't like? They were the same people who wanted you to try the dessert you didn't want. Really, come on, try it, they said, holding out the fork. Was it the desire to share? Was it power? Did they want the consolation of agreement, so they might feel, like these protesters, part of a larger connection? They were the same people who told you what you didn't want in a man. Or were they in fact the saintly ones, trying to protect you from what you seemed unable to register as dangerous? *You don't want that.*

But they didn't know the cliff of him, arriving in her small doorway.

Thanks, said the librarian flatly, taking the book with a mustard-colored fingerless glove.

This a lending library? Ivy said. The question came like a gush, so grateful was she to address something outside her head. She hadn't spoken to another person since noon when she'd left Nicky—it was a school half day—with the sitter for the afternoon.

The woman, lustrous hair piled in a bun on her head, looked put out. Her look said, Obviously.

So you take book donations? Long quiet hours had been part of her days for more than thirty years now, but she could never get used to the disorientation of reentering the world.

Again an irritated nod from the librarian.

So this is an honor system? Ivy asked.

We have a sign-up sheet. The woman's attitude said, Go away.

In the days after she saw him, everything she looked at would take on his perspective, or at least the perspective she imagined, as if his face were a mask on the inside of her skull. Was she compensating for his absence? It was involuntary. She did feel he had a sharper way of looking at things than she did, he was decidedly less of a fool. Taking on his perspective gave her a new and inspiring angle on things. Trees, for instance. Trees were something she'd always loved, but now trees were more fascinating than ever. Their enormous trunks with their crusty bark, the rings of wood, all from a tiny seed! And the branches spraying themselves out, governed by nothing but the need to grow, spreading in a perfect but unplanned design, producing one veined leaf after another, at perfectly placed yet random intervals, needing light, dropping off in the fall etc. etc. The miracle of trees! The miracle of them kept smacking her, even in this city covered with concrete and tar, trees were sprouting out of bucket-sized areas of actual earth. They had never spoken of trees, but somehow she felt the man had given her an increased amazement about trees.

A gust blew from above and blue pamphlets swam past her feet like ocean skates. Everything was like something else. In front of her a small sign in orange neon: WE WANT OUR COUNTRY BACK BITCHES. She turned down the sloping hill to leave.

•

Then on the far side of the park through curling spaces she saw a familiar line of neck and shoulder in a brown fatigue jacket. Her heart started up crazily, and instinct made her turn away. Jesus, she was even hallucinating him. Then like a bad spy, she pretended to search her pockets for something while glancing over her shoulder. He was on the other side of a row of trees, his back to her, talking to a woman with a hatchet chin and a ribbed vest, interviewing her. A man wearing a hooded sweatshirt and holding a camera on his shoulder filmed them. Ivy moved and nearly stepped on a person sleeping curled under a blanket of blurry blue and white snowflakes. The man had on a black wool hat and Ivy had never seen the shape of his head in a hat. It did not look familiar. No, she realized, it wasn't him. This man was thinner and his shoulders more narrow and his head was big for his body and he had the beginnings of a beard. Fleming was clean-shaven. At least, he had been when she'd last seen him.

Her hair blew into her mouth. Thin leaves swam like minnows in the air. The beard had a reddish tinge though. Maybe it was him. He. She backtracked to get a better angle. From there she saw she had definitely been wrong. This man was much smaller, and the hat was simply like one everyone else was wearing. The tilt of his neck toward the woman, listening, gathering information, though, that did look like Fleming. But Fleming was much taller and wider, she thought.

She stayed at a distance, up the hill, spying. Even watching this man not he, she felt the little stabs of his being somewhere that didn't include her. He was, in each and every moment, choosing not to be with her. This sort of line of thought threw her very quickly into a state of pain. Stop it, she told herself. Think of the good things. She wouldn't be able to keep him if she did not keep thinking of the good things.

The cameraman in the hoodie moved, blocking her view. He lowered his camera, and the man's face was straight in her direction. No, not him at all. It was a man who resembled him, but the features were not in his proportion, as if a child had arranged them, the way Nicky did with Mr. Potato Head. The man's brow seemed indented and his eyes shallow like wax melted. It was even creepy, his mouth starved and thin, not at all the mouth she knew, plump and lovely to kiss. Amazed at the eerie coincidence she kept glancing furtively at this half-matching person. He appeared to be scouting around for the next thing to film, his ear tipped to the cameraman, conferring. Only a narrow tree trunk was blocking his line of vision to her but he wasn't looking in her direction.

For a split second she thought about walking by him, to see up close this doppelgänger. But something kept her away. She wasn't prepared to present herself to anyone at the moment, not feeling particularly appealing: pale, wind whipped, drained.

Well, she was relieved it wasn't he. In the afternoons arriving at his black-and-white apartment she would feel gleaming, expectant, ready to present her body to him. She trudged now toward the top of the park where police barricades of blue sawhorses made a low fence marking the official edge of the encampment. She watched her legs walking, but saw instead the window in his white room where the daylight made a radiant rim around the rice-paper blinds. She saw herself encased in the glass shower with the beads of water clinging and him stepping in that first time, unembarrassed, saying, Excuse me, with a matter-of-fact air, as if the rollicking and tumultuous hours they'd just had in bed were an everyday occurrence, familiar and regular for him. This seemed to her a sign both good and bad, good in how he was an unhurried and warm lover, and bad in how little if any impact it seemed to have. Excuse me, he had said, reaching past her to a bar of soap. It was easy to be unembarrassed when one felt nothing at stake. She passed a dog-eyed man carrying a cardboard holder with four cups of coffee bearing the stamp of the Starbucks maiden. The man swerved gracefully to give Ivy room to pass. Thanks, she said. Sorry.

Sorry.

Somewhere the bright sun went behind a cloud and the buildings darkened, altering the mood. At a bench bolted to the ground, she stepped up between some cartons of food cans for a higher view. The cameraman in the hoodie and the man had not moved but had turned their backs, looking for new victims. A shiver ran through her; it was colder up here. Her coat was too thin. No, not him, but what if it had been?

A dull rope of despair pulled at her lower ribs. Or maybe it was just fatigue. One hit these bland pockets of exhaustion a couple of times a day and just had to forge on through them. Usually they happened at the playground as she was watching—

She looked at her watch. Shit. Twenty-five past five. She jumped off the bench and walked briskly toward the nearest exit and half ran up the street to her bike. She was going to be late. The blue Schwinn was splayed sideways off the post, someone had knocked it over. Half the time one returned to a locked bike dislodged by—what? A car? An angry person kicking it over for fun? The bike was rusted and trashed anyway so it hardly mattered, one gear wire sprouted in front like an antenna. She kept it locked out on the street, since there was no room in the tiny apartment. There was barely enough room for two people. She'd converted the shoebox-sized study into a shoebox-sized bedroom for Nicky. The apartment was meant, really, for one person.

On her bike she glided down the one-way street, the tire spoke

clicking against something broken or out of place. She purposefully did not look in the direction of the hoodied cameraman and
his director. Her attention now was required to be on her son. She
was the one person on earth looking out for him, and a loosening
of that vigilance would result in who knows what manner of harm
and recklessness. Every now and then she was struck by the pre-
cariousness of her duty, how much his life hinged on hers, how
she was the sole person on the earth, really, tending to this helpless creature, and her brain would often reel thinking of all the
children as helpless who did not have someone they could rely on.
She had managed to avoid that hinged life for years, though she
had serially hinged with a number of men. But then she would
unhinge. Unhinging was not something you could ever do with
a child.

A herd of people poured into the crosswalk at the bottom of
the street, seemingly ignoring the encampment in the park. The
pedestrians walking quickly took it for granted that they would all
avoid one another. Everyone was used to it. But Ivy found it amazing how each person managed to avoid knocking into another,
a sort of cooperative behavior as mysterious, really, as those sil-
very fish in colossal schools which swept in one direction then
another, hundreds of them, so fast, so expertly in time. People
with their unspoken cooperation were as amazing as trees. She
canoed along with one foot oaring the ground.

Traffic was at a standstill; horns honked. A white van at her
elbow inched forward, staying just far enough to the right by the
curb so she could not pass.

Impatience flushed her chest and into her forehead: once
again she would be late. Once again it was her fault. The aware-

ness of her being to blame caused more anxiousness than the lateness itself. Ahead in a wide crosswalk made vast by the crater's blocked-off streets, a traffic cop in an orange-and-yellow vest addressed the gridlock, moving her arms like a proud conductor. Cars lurched forward at her wave, then stopped again in the jam.

Ivy dismounted. Cars with blinking lights hugged the curb. The space between the cars was too narrow, so she humped her wheels onto the sidewalk, swerving urgently. People had decidedly less respect for a pushed bicycle than they did for another human and she wove past irritated glances and people stepping to the side with mild outrage. A bike was not supposed to be on the sidewalk. Drivers in cars seemed to feel the same way about the bikes on the road. Bikes were welcomed nowhere.

Off the curb, back onto the road, she swung up onto the seat, pedaled across at the stoplight and glided along a traffic-less area cleared for construction. No people walked here. Orange cones dotted in front of a skyscraper whose lower floors were walls of glass and upper floors a skeleton in steel. She pedaled furiously along the vacant square, gaining momentum, and was startled by a construction worker in suspenders who stepped out from behind a shed and jumped back just in time to avoid being hit by her.

Hey, he screamed in a deep street voice. She sped by, no time for him. You idiot, he called. You're going to hurt someone!

He was right. She was being reckless. But she wasn't going to say sorry this time, she thought, she was in a hurry for a reason, she had her little boy—even if this time saying sorry would have actually been appropriate. She pumped the pedals, ignoring his cry, trying to ignore her responsibility. It felt familiar, the determination to ignore. And nearly choking at her throat came an eruption of rage toward Dexter Fleming—for not being there, for having captured her interest, and then for keeping her so damn preoccupied. A wave of exhausted shame crashed over her. The screaming man was right, she was an absolute idiot.

Her eyes shut against the shame of it as she whizzed beside an untouched concrete sidewalk and slanted around the corner. In front of her, a patch of road the size of a coffin had been dug up and refilled with sharp cubes of granite. It was a surprise and too close. She would skid if she turned on it and before she'd even had the thought she squeezed the hand brake, the one that worked, and her front tire stopped on a dime. The bike froze upright, and Ivy pitched flying forward over the handlebars, her arms behind winglike, aware in the microsecond of the flight that this was going to be either really bad, or okay. She was going to be either slightly hurt, or have a major disaster, possibly be maimed for life. She even flashed on an ICU with monitors beeping and her body lying with a mask on its face. She flashed too on Nicky swinging on his monkey bars, his gaze past his tiny arms, checking to see she was watching. She even saw her ex-husband, Henry, forehead wrinkled with concern, a rare expression he reserved for important moments.

Her chin landed first, with the sound of two rocks hitting each other. A white, then black, strobe swept through her head. She crumpled into a lump on the cold tar. A fizzing numbness spiked through her body at the same time a burning sensation raked the left side of her face. She pushed up on one arm, relieved she could move and sit and turn her head. The wind was knocked out of her, but her neck didn't seem to be broken, though there was a worrying ache across her jaw. Was her throat closing up? She turned her torso in slow motion to see the angry construction worker striding toward her. She touched her chin, felt wetness, and saw the red black drips down the front of her green canvas coat.

You okay? the man bellowed.

She lifted her unpropped arm and waved it stiffly, like a wisp of grass, unable to speak. Nothing was inside her. She was suspended, stopped. She saw other figures approaching. She felt an odd relief. For a few moments at least she would not be required to do anything . . . she had only to tend to this, this accident. She was involuntarily occupied. A woman in a colorful coat appeared at her side. She was older, dark skinned, with hair cropped in a corn yellow cap. Can you hear me? the woman said with a reassuring lack of condescension. Good. You're okay. Now don't you worry, we'll get you help.

Another figure, a portly man in a blue jogging suit, stood above her. Don't move, he said, breathing deeply. They're calling 911. He gestured mysteriously back in the direction of the park. She had to be only here.

Nicky, though. She had to get word to Nicky. As soon as she could speak she would get someone to call the sitter. No, she'd get them to call Irene, and Irene would step into action and know just what to do and would fetch Nicky and bring him back to her happy house with the twins and the dogs and the husband, doing it all effortlessly because Irene was capable and knew how to care and look after these things.

Her perspective for a moment zoomed up above and looked down at the scene from a height: she saw the colorful coat, a jogger in his blue outfit, the suspendered construction worker in his cap, and herself like a splotch on the ground at the center. She was rarely in the center. Surrounded by these strangers she felt a peculiar sense of bliss. The sky seemed to widen.

As she sat, catching her breath, she observed the crowd gathering around her. Random thoughts came, like candles lit on a river. How would it be if Mr. Fleming were here? Might it awaken in him a feeling for her he'd not yet had? She recognized it as a pathetic thought, but that didn't stop more embarrassing thoughts from coming. She had a quick vision of him visiting her as she lay in bed . . . in the hospital? No, in her bedroom. He would not be bothered by the fact that the side of her face looked like raw beef. He couldn't be shocked. That was consoling. He probably was so tough nothing could hurt him. The visit would bring them closer, perhaps to something real. That is what she wanted, after all: real. She didn't know if he had it in him though: to want something real.

In the moments after the impact, everything inside was oddly clear, as if everything extraneous inside her were gone. All the jumping worry, all those heavy pellets of pain. Her internal activity switched from thinking to breathing. A sense of only wonder prevailed.

·

Sometimes an accident cleared the horizon. She felt like a giant brass gong that had been hit, then saw the healthy vessel of herself frozen in shock at how she'd allowed herself to be unprotected, that she'd flung herself out without the least care for the damage it might do, to herself or to another. She would never have been so reckless with her son, but with herself . . . Well, it was easier to care about a person not oneself.

Vibrating with clarity, she saw her son's face looking steeply up from his position on the rug as it had so often been when she walked in, his neck retracted, his open gaze receiving her as if she were a column of light entering the room, and in the brightness she realized that of course it was Dexter Fleming back there. The person resembled him because he was the person. She had not been hallucinating. It was exactly he. Her view of him had never been from a distance, it had always been up close. From afar, his face was dented and flat and traumatized. It was the face of a person who cared little to nothing about her.

She was receiving more care from the woman in a colorful coat, from the angry construction worker, and from the passing jogger with his matter-of-fact gut, than it seemed she'd ever gotten from the man, and all the lines connecting her to him, the erotic and the intriguing, the smart and the electric, seemed to snap one at a time as if ripped away in a gale wind, easily detached because there was nothing tested binding them.

•

Come on, came a voice, and some assured hands were lifting her at the armpits. Let's get you up.

She let herself be lifted, and shakily stood.

One needed people's help. One needed people. A lift from a person helped you picture things as okay.

The arms helping her along were in a white uniform. She turned to the face. It was close up: dark-skinned and smooth with a mustache. The man's downcast eyes were studying the problem of her, eyes doing his job. She saw a white ambulance van waiting with its open back doors and glanced back to her crumpled bicycle. The jogger had righted it and held it by the handlebars. He gave her a thumbs-up, sending her off. Who knows what he was going to do with it, but she felt reassured he was taking care of it. She saw the cave where she lived being illuminated and even saw an exit at the back. She didn't want to be in a cave anymore. She didn't want to be in a black-and-white room. Its allure was gone. She still felt clear inside. As the pain in her jaw thickened her throat she thought, I must keep this clarity. For Nicky. The thought repeated: Keep this clarity. The lack of allure. She prayed to remember it. She must take it in and let it occupy her.

Here we go, said the man's voice, guiding her to a stretcher which had snapped up nearby. The guiding hand made her feel as if she were in a fairy tale being led to a tower. There you are, said the voice and lowered her onto a crinkling mattress.

Okay, she thought, lying back. She gazed up at the man's face with its strong dark forehead and thought, Okay, whatever you say. Take me.

And she moved from one version of surrender to another.

· GREEN GLASS ·

"Will you-know-who be at the wedding?" Fran said.

"Yes," Tom said, reading the paper. "She will."

"You know?" Fran stood in the doorway that led to the narrow kitchen slot.

"Yes, she called me. The other day."

"She called you again?" Fran came out into the room. The apartment had one other small room, just big enough for the bed. "She was the one who left you," Fran said. "Why doesn't she act like it?"

Fran turned back into the narrow slot of kitchen. "She should act like it."

"She did not leave me," Tom said. "It was a mutual decision. Things had been over long before she left."

"Did *you* leave?" Fran said.

Tom shrugged. "She just happened to mention it first."

"I don't see why she calls you all the time," Fran said.

"She does not call me all the time." Tom put down the paper.

"Enough, she does."

"She's a friend. We've known each other a long time."

"A friend?" Fran said.

"Yes, a friend. That's what it was like. That's why it didn't last."

"Six years is a pretty long time for it not to last," Fran said.

"We weren't together the whole time," Tom said. "We broke up a lot."

"And got back together every time," Fran said.

"I felt guilty," Tom said.

"Right."

"I did. And we had a lot in common."

"Like what?"

"I don't know. Reading. She liked books. Liked animals." Tom hesitated—dangerous territory. "We got along well."

"I'm surprised you let her go." Fran stirred onions in a frying pan.

"Frannie," Tom said.

"Really. Getting along so beautifully—and liking to read. That is rare."

"You're being ridiculous," Tom said.

Fran was quiet. Tom came into the narrow kitchen.

"Listen, I'm sorry she calls me. I can't do anything about it."

"You can't?" Fran turned astonished eyes on Tom.

"What?" Tom said. "You want me to tell her not to call?"

"I'm not going to tell you what to do." Fran pushed the onions this way and that with a wooden spoon.

"If you want that," Tom said, "you should say so."

"I just don't like it," Fran said. "Isn't it all right just to not like it?"

"I'll tell her not to call," Tom said, giving up. He looked out the window to the flat tops of buildings at different heights. "But she won't understand."

"Of course she'll understand," Fran said. "Not that you should do it. She just doesn't want to let you go."

Tom regarded Fran with pity. "She's not like that. She's not as sensitive as you are."

"Men like to think women aren't sensitive, at convenient times."

"Maybe I know her better than you do," Tom said.

"Are you saying she doesn't have strong feelings?"

"Come on, honey." Tom stood behind Fran and pulled her to him. "Why are we talking about this? I love you."

"I just don't understand how you could have been with that person all that time," Fran said softly.

"It's pointless to think about," Tom said into her hair.

"It's not voluntary," Fran murmured. "It's a feeling."

•

Sunlight filled the windows of the chapel, and light green leaves threw a leafy pattern of shade over the empty pews in front.

"You know all these people?" Fran said.

"Mostly on Buster's side," Tom said. "Some of the bride's."

"A lot of blonds," Fran said.

"A lot of marriages," Tom said. "Buster's family alone could fill this chapel, if you included all the divorces."

"What's with that guy?" Fran said.

Tom followed her gaze. "Mr. Hildreth. He hasn't had his daily ration of cocktails yet."

Fran watched the people entering the arching door. She turned abruptly and faced forward. "Guess who," she said. Tom glanced back. Fran toyed with the hem at her knees. She'd worn a black print vintage dress. "Where's she sitting?" she said.

"Don't worry," Tom said. "Way back on the other side."

"I'm not worried. I'm just wondering."

After a few minutes, Fran shot a look over her shoulder. "Oh, she looks good. Carefully avoiding our direction. Who's she with?"

"That's Heidi and Hilary. They're all friends of the bride."

"Old home week," Fran said.

"They're nice, actually. I like Heidi and Hilary."

"I'm sure you do," Fran said.

"Honey."

"Sorry." Fran took Tom's hand into her lap. "I just feel a little out of it. Maybe I shouldn't have come."

"I wanted you to."

"I wanted to too. But you know what I mean."

"Don't worry about it," Tom said.

The organ music changed from something jaunty to something serious, and the groom appeared at the front of the chapel by the purple-and-white spray of flowers. He was biting his lower lip, possibly joking, possibly sincere. It was hard to tell. The bridesmaids in lilac passed down the aisle, with unrelenting smiles, balancing purple garlands on their heads. The bride followed, on the arm of a man she kept at a distance.

"What's that thing sticking out of her rear?" Fran whispered.

The sermon focused on the sacred qualities of marriage. The trembling of the bride's veil could be seen from the back pew.

Soon the organ hit the staccato chords of the wedding march

and the couple flew out the door. Outside, the late afternoon was tranquil and bright. Tom and Fran strolled down a slope to stand apart and watch the members of the wedding party arranging themselves for a photographer. People milled around.

"Tommy Stanwyck!" A woman in a wide-brimmed hat engulfed Tom in yellow polka dots. "Where are your parents? So naughty of them not to have come. Is this your girlfriend? Fran? So nice to meet you. Didn't I see your *old* flame up there, Tommy?" The woman winked at Fran. "I've got *two* exes here—two out of four! Don't give it a thought . . ." The woman sputtered away.

Fran glanced back up to the church. "Maybe we should go say hi to her. Get it over with."

"Okay." Tom took her arm and they started up the hill.

•

On the way to the reception, they drove behind a car that had Heidi and Hilary in the back seat, with a familiar head in between.

"That was the shortest dress I've ever seen," Fran said.

"It looked ridiculous," Tom said, hands firmly on the steering wheel.

"If you've got the body, why not?" Fran said weakly.

"To a wedding?"

"You know," Fran said, "I thought she looked kind of sad. My heart went out to her." Fran watched the placid countryside go by.

Tom drove, eyes straight ahead.

"She seems different from how you talk about her," Fran said.

"You may not be the best judge," Tom said.

"I don't think she seems hard at all," Fran said.

"I didn't say she was hard. I said she wasn't that sensitive."

"She looked sensitive just now," Fran said. "I've never seen anyone go so white."

"When?" Tom said, but something else was bothering him.

"Just now. Outside the church. She looked terrified."

"She was a little embarrassed," Tom said stiffly. "It's understandable. I don't think anyone would think it strange for it to be a little embarrassing seeing the new girlfriend."

"What did you think?" Fran said. "'Here's a person I spent six years of my life with'?"

"I didn't think anything." Tom bent to turn on the radio. "It was a little awkward is all."

"I think she has a certain dignity about her." Fran stared at the car in front of them gliding around wide corners under the ceiling of trees. "With that long neck. Isn't there something sort of regal about her?"

"I don't know." Tom found a station with music and left it on.

"Haven't you ever noticed that?" Fran turned down the volume.

"No."

"Makes me feel like a dwarf," Fran said.

"Stop it," Tom said sharply.

"I mean it. If I were you, I'd rather be with her."

"You are insane," Tom said, angry. "I'm not in love with her."

Fran looked out the window. "I can't imagine why not."

"You don't need to," Tom said. "It's got nothing to do with you."

"She's been with you so much longer than I have," Fran said. "I hate that."

"Why do you want to make yourself unhappy?" Tom said.

"I don't," Fran said. "What were you like with her?"

"That has nothing to do with us."

"What if I found out you were a member of the Ku Klux Klan before I met you—wouldn't that have something to do with us?"

"You're losing your mind," Tom said.

"Wouldn't it?"

"I don't know what you are talking about."

"Why won't you answer me?" Fran said.

"Because it's the question of an insane person."

They rode along in silence, past stone walls crumbling in the slanted light and ponds with green glassy surfaces.

"You never had fights like this with her, did you?"

"No," Tom said matter-of-factly. "It wasn't like that."

"How could you not have fights?" Fran said. "Was she too above it?"

"I don't know," Tom said wearily.

"You must think I'm so—so petty compared with her." Fran took some combs out of her hair and put them back in.

"Please," Tom said.

"I'm just letting out my feelings." Fran tried a few times to set the combs right. "I don't know what else to do with them."

"Keep them in," Tom said. After a moment he added, looking at Fran's stony profile, "That's a joke."

·

Night fell over the reception at the country club. Tom and Fran stepped down from the slate terrace onto a golf green. At the edge of the light, figures strolled into the darkness.

"So how do you know that lawyer guy?" Tom said.

"Who, Alex?" Fran said. "From around."

"Do you always kiss guys you know from around?"

"Well, I sort of . . ." Fran's voice trailed off.

Tom halted in his tracks. "Did you go out with him?"

"Sort of." Fran laughed. "Brief thing."

"You *went out* with that jerk?"

"Tom, you don't even know him."

"Yes, I do. Everybody knows him. He's a complete slimeball. How could you go out with him?"

Fran didn't answer.

"He's known for getting drug dealers out of jail and screwing models!"

"It didn't last long," Fran said. "Obviously." She looked through the clubhouse windows and saw Buster, the groom, at one end of the room and his bride at the other. "It was a short thing."

"But what were you doing with him at all?" Tom had become shrill.

"Let's drop it," Fran said.

"Oh, we can talk about my past but not about yours?"

"I thought you didn't ever want to hear anything about my past," Fran said.

"I don't."

"Good. Then drop it."

"Okay." Tom folded his arms. "As soon as you tell me what you saw in that asshole."

"Jesus," Fran said. "Believe it or not, he did have some good qualities." Then she shook her head. "Listen, it never should have happened."

"You're so gullible," Tom said with disgust. "All a man has to do is say a few complimentary things and you completely fall for it. Women are such fools."

"Excuse me, but I don't recall ever having told you what went on."

"I know what guys like that are like." Tom faced into the darkness.

"Okay. It was a mistake." Fran reached up to his shoulder. "Haven't you ever made a mistake?"

"Not with an asshole," Tom said, turning to her.

"Come on," Fran said gently. "Let's stop. Let's go in and eat. Go see how Buster is."

"Who's hungry?" Tom said.

•

It was after ten when they left the reception.

"Are you going to sulk all the way home?" Fran said.

Their headlights wove through the blackness.

"If I don't talk, does that mean I'm sulking?"

"No."

After a while Fran said, "So, did you have a good time?"

"Yup."

"You don't sound too enthusiastic."

"I had a fine time," Tom said. "One of my oldest friends just got married to a cream puff. It was a nice wedding. Leave me alone."

They drove for a while.

"Can I ask if you talked to her?"

"Yes."

"Did you?"

"Yes."

"Well, how was it?" Fran said.

"She slapped me," said Tom.

"She what?"

"She slapped me. Across the face." Tom began to look happier.

"Why?" Fran asked with astonishment.

"I don't know. She must have been angry with something I said."

"Obviously," Fran said. She gazed up at Tom, waiting, but he didn't speak. "So?" she said finally.

"So what?" Tom said innocently.

"What did you say to her to make her hit you?" Fran enunciated each word.

"Don't know." Tom shrugged. "I guess it was something about her dress."

"What was it?"

"I told her she looked like a hooker."

"You didn't."

Tom nodded. "Then she slapped me."

"That wasn't a very nice thing to say," Fran whispered.

"She didn't seem to think so either," Tom said. "Oh, God, now what? Are you crying?"

"It upsets me."

"Why?"

"It just does."

"Okay, okay. Calm down."

Fran pressed herself against the door of the car. "She does care. She obviously does. I knew she did!"

"It's the past," Tom said. "You can't do anything about the past. Forget about it."

"It happened now." She sobbed and put her forehead to the black window. "I'm not thinking about the past. I'm thinking about the future."

"The future?" Tom tried to glimpse her face as headlights came toward them and flashed past.

"Ours."

"You're insane," Tom said.

"You always say that." Fran was suddenly hushed. She looked at Tom. "Why do you always say that?"

"I don't."

"You do. A lot."

"Maybe because you act insane," Tom said. "Where do you get these ideas?"

"They're not ideas, they're feelings." Fran straightened her back, attempting to compose herself. "Why did you say that to her?"

"Because it was true." Tom lifted his hand in the shape of a spade.

Fran stared at him for a long time. "If you two had gotten married, a lot of those people would have been at the wedding, wouldn't they?"

"We were never going to get married," Tom said.

"Yes, but if you had."

"Not a lot of them." Tom thought a moment. "Some."

"I bet she was thinking that, too." Fran looked out at the black night, once and yet still green.

"I doubt it. She does have another boyfriend, you know."

"Why wasn't he there?"

"Buster didn't invite him," Tom said.

"Why not?"

"He doesn't approve," Tom said. "He thinks the guy is sleazy."

Fran laughed bitterly. "Ha. Buster probably liked her himself."

"Actually," Tom said, and the thought made him smile. "Not that long ago, he did."

· WHY I DON'T WRITE ·

What do you do all day? she said.

In the morning, there is the counter with the teapot and the bag of tea in the white cup, the milk from the carton in the fridge door, the chair, which chair, the paper, the notebook, which notebook, the folder, the letters on the screen, the emails asking, the computer keyboard—then it all stops.

She handed me the paper. "Here's the bad news," she said.

It takes courage to be happy.

The headlines:
FINGERS POINT, DENIALS SPREAD AND FURY RISES
THE PUFFIN VANISHES
SUPREME COURT NOMINEE CHALLENGED
SYRIAN FORCES HAVE CONFLICTING REPORTS

I read parts of them, read the whole article through of: the suicide of a dancer who jumped off a building on the Upper West Side.

On the page in front of me in ink: *The road shot forward like
an arrow disappearing in the clouds between a bluff and rocky hills.*

Before waking I found a deep slash in my upper arm; out of
the opening floated small lobsters.

Overheard: Telling someone your goal makes it less likely to
happen.

He went off his medication.

The morning dishes, the tacky slick on the shelf, the flicker-
ing light, the cabinet door slipped off its hinge, the rotted sill, the
curling screen.

Your system must be overloaded. Or you have a virus.

Where was the daughter? She was frozen, head bent down,
her face awash in a light blue glow as if spotlit by aliens. Her finger flicked over the screen like a conductor.

What shall we have for dinner? More eggs.

Sponge. Lemon. Milk.

I used to be ruled by feeling; it asked for words.

What's going on with the weather.

What are you looking at? I ask my daughter staring at the phone.
Why do you care?
Just wondering what's going into your brain.
Mom, leave me alone.

Arthur Rimbaud gave up writing poetry at age twenty-one.

During the sad movie I feel a pain spread in my chest, becoming so sharp I felt I was having a heart attack.

Where was the daughter? What time was the doctor?
What was eaten?
What was smoked?
What made her cry?
She was late. She told a lie.
She was beautiful and laughing.

Take fifteen minutes out of the day.

I walk on an empty road at dusk. Far off on the water I hear a boat humming. I hear the flute call of a loon. Then silence.

Something dripping. Life is not right.

We hope you will make it. We'd love to see you. It's been too long. Shall we meet for lunch? Let's have that drink. You should come to Copenhagen. There's a two fifty-five show. I have an extra ticket for tomorrow. The lines aren't too long. You have to see it. You have to watch it. You have to read it.

Your balance total is—

All day you ask yourself, What are you doing all day?

Fifty-three dead not including the shooter.

When you take the plant out of the plastic container, pull the thin roots to dangle down and place into the hole. Give it water.

Tunnel, no light at the end of. One hour, then another.

The title of the song: "Crawl to Me, Baby, Crawl to Me."

Are you going to the march?

As soon as you gave them a donation, they bombarded you with continual requests for more.

They heard back from the doctor: it was not good news.

That's not what the fire marshal said.

I walk around the city and listen to people as I pass them on sidewalks. Usually they are talking on their phones. Often they are not looking at where they are going; they are looking into their palms.

"You are in the wrong line; your line is over there."

The sweet air in the morning, warmed by the sun.

She slammed the door and the molding cracked. How many coats of paint the wood had gotten was amazing.

Headache.

Hunger.

The thumping far below the floor.

Death estimates ran from 150 to 500, but could not be confirmed.

You write if you have to.

The spine of a book, sugarcane yellow with an embossed palm tree half hooked in a circle. Pages with deckle edge. The first line: *In March 1912, when a big mail-boat was unloading in Naples, there was an accident about which extremely inaccurate reports appeared in the newspapers . . .*
You read eagerly on, hopeful.

Cleaning out the closets. Cleaning out the drawers. Clearing out the basement.

We used to be friends.

Beckett's "I can't go on."
Then his: "I'll go on . . ."
But

Suicide by hanging. Just an hour before, the designer had been—

Housing rates, fiscal responsibility, sleep deprivation.

I'll bring some coconut rice; you bring your pie.

He didn't show up.

Payment details. Tuition total. Balance due.

The kids are exhausted.

Marinate it in the soy, oil, garlic, sugar mixture.

Caring used to have a ragged pain, sometimes wafty, sometimes sharp as needles. Its magnet weight kept me connected.

For a long time I would return to the black-and-white room.

Sorry. Sorry. Sorry.

The one with the wedge heel. The striped linen. A pair with a high waist.

Probably three years ago.
No, actually it was seven.

More garbage bags.

Didn't you see it on Instagram?

Before he died, he was screaming for painkillers.

Will be subject to late fees.

"Nobody's going to leave themselves too exposed right now," said the man on his phone. He paused at the corner and repeated it. "Nobody's going to leave themselves too exposed right now."

The keys have to be replaced.

I haven't seen him in over twenty years.

An hour ago, I felt calm, now I am heartbroken with worry. Is it the dentist? Is it the daughter's distress? Is it death?

"Come to bed."

Open any page of Emily Dickinson and have the top of your head taken off.

No one saying, "Come to bed."

She died, God, is it already ten years ago? It was awful. Death used to be more awful. One was destroyed.

You saw him? How was he?
He was great. Looked older though.

It was hard to explain. So I gave up.

He got another one, prettier, younger.

A child watches his dad lose his patience: the look in the child's eye.

Only in tomorrow night, hope you are free. Where do you have to be? Where are you coming from?

Wish I could see him.

Looks better ironed.

The woman turning the corner: I used to wear my hair like that.

He was found slumped on the floor, having put on one sneaker, about to go running.

Another story became more important.

Wish I could go there.

How delicious is that?

It didn't matter anymore.

Is this as unbelievable as I think it is?

At dinner they all laughed and laughed and the next day she couldn't remember what had been so funny.

Gazes used to slide off me.

She had a temperature of 102.7.

"I don't read it anymore."

The ways that Bob Dylan says
1. He's all right, and
2. He's not all right.

I passed her on our street. She didn't see me, she was looking at the flowers.

"I don't read anymore."

Taste this.

A FINAL TURN OFF NOTICE IS IN EFFECT.

I see a cupped hand inside me as if through layers of bullet-proof Plexiglas. It's there, but it isn't in charge.

"I don't believe it anymore."

Did you ever apologize?

Star-splashed sky. Wind in the grass. Butterfly. Bee seeming to be in fast motion, burrowing in a flower. A flower you never saw before.

The cat hissed. Probably four to six more years to live.

Wasn't asked back.

Chekhov, doctor. Virginia Woolf, mental struggles.

The drain is clogged and I need to replace the broken—

Come to bed.

Despite having said the opposite thing that morning . . .
Denied that he knew . . .
Denied he had said . . .

"I don't look anymore."

The recipe in last week's—

Suspension of service.

Forgetting I met him.
Forgetting the weekend. Not meaning to be hurtful.
Forgetting to show up for the meeting.

I heard they were sharing a boat down the Nile. I heard they went to Algeria. I wondered, When did they make these plans with each other?

You figure: about twenty more good years. You feel something strange.

"Was that the IPA or the Pilsner?"

Passing a man who holds your gaze!

At lunch one of the people returns the bill to the small tray. "We each owe eighty-five dollars," she announces.

Passing stylish people speaking French.

"You're a woman. Why would you think that?"

What's going on with this cold, with this heat, with this rain.

He slept on his side next to the bank vent. Or was it a she?

I was choking with rage and at the end of the plank where my grief walked I finally stepped off and the weeping stopped. All was calm. I was blank and numb.

"We couldn't be happier."
"We're all full up."

Why are we here?

The impact killed her instantly.

Sorry, I have other plans.

The cool air at night.

Lucky to be alive. A miracle to be alive.

You write if without it you would die.

In the morning passing a man and a woman kissing each other goodbye, leaning onto each other, drawing strength for the day.

Beethoven getting loud, Beethoven getting soft.

Never see enough of you.

Is this as unbelievable as I think it is?

All men do that. Not worth worrying.

With extra whipped cream, please.

Wetting a watercolor cube. Touching the paintbrush to stiff paper.

Tolstoy.

Women writers without children: many. Women writers with children: few.

Use of the drug was up 33 percent in the last six months.

Can't you take a joke?

My friend says, "Vibrationally I think it's easier to move forward if we stick to the truth."

Shakespeare.

No need to make up anything. The world will up you.

Another loss. Will lose again. Each time you feel it more. Each time you feel it less.

You can get those removed, you know. It's not *that* expensive.

Wallace Stevens, insurance man. Nabokov: lepidopterist. Goethe: horticulturalist.

The lights go down. The curtain opens. The comets streak.

Medication made all the difference.

Frank Sinatra suddenly singing in Starbucks from another world.

He didn't get back to me.

Watched the second season.

spinach
sesame oil
maple syrup
oranges/apples
milk

His statement contradicted the truth.

The drain clogged again. Something else more important.

While dying, he took no painkillers.

Tree branches flashing by the car window. The beauty.

Jane Austen. Flannery O'Connor. The Brontë sisters. Husbands?

Need new socks. New underwear. Tomorrow.

Of the billions of creatures alive today and of the billions of creatures who have lived, not one has come up with an adequate explanation of why we are here.

I watch my daughter dance with a frown on her face and a warm feeling washes across my chest.

Dust haloing the lampshade.

On her deathbed, she said in a shaky voice, "We had a good time, didn't we?"

The pipes are shot. Need to be redone.

Another story will come.

See above.

"But you can't leave," cried Isabel when she spotted Bonnie and George getting into their coats in the bright hall. She hurried toward them, knees locked, arms thrown down in outrage. Bonnie and George smiled at her sheepishly.

"We had a lovely time," Bonnie said.

"Dinner was delicious," said George.

"You two are no fun anymore," Isabel said. "Falling in love is antisocial."

George gazed around him, as if trying to recall something. Being tall he regarded objects near the ground as possibly too far away to bother with. "Did you see where I put my . . . ?"

Bonnie smiled up at him.

"You two are ridiculous," said Isabel. She lit a cigarette. "I never should have introduced you."

George wandered off into another room. He was the sort of person who didn't always remember people's names, who didn't worry about being on time for a plane. Bonnie was spellbound by his lack of anxiety. She had worries that plagued her—how to get by on her teaching salary, what was going to happen when the lease was up, how to put something fine into the world. Being near George was like sitting unconcerned on a cloud.

Bonnie kissed Isabel on the cheek. She would be happy to stay—Isabel was a dear friend and normally she'd have been there to the end, helping Isabel clean up and talking about who had been at dinner—but she was just as happy to go. She found a new satisfaction in doing what George wanted to do. Was she giving herself up? Was she turning herself over to him? She didn't care.

"I'm sorry Richard got here so late," Bonnie said, remembering to think of Isabel's feelings.

Isabel shrugged, but showed it had bothered her. Richard worked too hard. "Par for the course," she said. Then brightly, "You wait, it will happen to you. When the first blush wears off . . ."

Bonnie nodded sleepily, hearing the words from far away. It was hard to imagine George letting work take over. Work, like many other things, seemed hardly to touch him. He rarely talked about what he did, treating it as something unconnected to his real life, something apart from *him*. One of the things Bonnie had liked about George when she first met him was exactly that: he was not overly concerned about his career. Somehow it made Bonnie feel all the more important to him. He was simply a person, engaged in the moment right in front of him. One felt he would do whatever he wanted whenever and however he wanted to do it. Earlier in the evening while Bonnie was helping peel potatoes in the narrow kitchen, Isabel had asked if Bonnie had figured out exactly what it was that George did. Bonnie gave the usual computer business explanation, sounding unconvincing—she didn't know much about either business or computers—and said that Isabel should just ask him herself.

"I've tried," Isabel said, and one eyebrow went up. "He won't tell me."

"Found it," George said and held up a knapsack. Isabel and Bonnie exchanged a look. The olive-green knapsack was torn and stained and George didn't notice, or didn't care. In the knapsack were the mysterious papers he carted around from office to office, doing consulting work. Bonnie, who taught English literature, understood little of what he'd told her, though some of the language was intriguing—optical chips, WORMS, Macintosh—while other language was not: multitasking systems, hypertext, Usenet. Sometimes he borrowed empty apartments to work in. He had ideas for projects of his own, but they were in an incubation stage, nothing ready to put into practice . . .

"Rushing back to their love haven," Isabel said. She caught sight of herself in the giant hall mirror—the apartment belonged to her stepmother who lived in Paris—and sucked in her cheeks and plucked at her bangs. "So tell me," she said, "how many times are you going to do it tonight?" She puffed on her cigarette, holding it up near her ear. "Come on, how many?"

Bonnie colored and smiled. She didn't know how to joke this way very well. "Just once," she said with a flippant tone, making no joke whatsoever. She didn't want to gloat. Isabel and Richard had not been having the best time lately in that department.

George's eyes glittered. He was an expert at being flippant, not inclined to take things too seriously, and he and Isabel joked often. "All night long though," he said. Bonnie liked being near their banter. It made her feel—well—not so serious.

George pressed the button for the elevator.

"How can you leave me?" Isabel cried. She grabbed Bonnie's sleeves, and gazed up at George. "You're abandoning me to the elections!" She glanced over her shoulder toward a glow of candles in the maroon darkness of the dining room. Past high candlesticks was Richard, tie loosened, leaning back in his chair, admiring a cigar. The man beside him—someone named Froy—was nodding, tossing a balled-up napkin into the air and catching it. A woman, headless because she was standing, poured coffee into Isabel's stepmother's china cups. "It could go on all night!" Isabel said with a withered expression.

"Too bad," George said. He put his leather motorcycle jacket on. "Work tomorrow."

"Work," Isabel said. "I bet you two have been getting a lot of work done lately. What do you do—call in sick?"

"Naturally," George said. Bonnie wondered idly whom he would call.

"Work has sort of fallen by the wayside," Bonnie said. Admitting it made the old worry resurface—the unread papers, the classes shoddily prepared for, the book review ignored. Before meeting George these were things she was diligent about. She looked up at his smooth face with no worry on it. How much energy she had wasted, for so long, on worrying! Her own expression softened again as if drugged. She hugged Isabel goodbye.

"You two are ridiculous," Isabel said again.

"And you are wonderful," said George. It was the perfect thing to say to Isabel. He kissed her good night. "Hey, great boots," he said, and she lifted her foot to be praised, "though nothing compared to the legs in them." Isabel beamed.

"I'm glad somebody notices my legs." Then she pouted. The elevator door opened, right there in the foyer, rousing her. "You can't leave me!" she cried.

"Evening, Isabel," said the man in the elevator.

"Oh, Mr. Buffy!" she cried. "I want to come with them. They're in love!"

Bonnie and George stepped into the elevator and waved at Isabel. The door slid shut. "Madly in love!" they heard behind it.

Mr. Buffy spoke, his voice gruff and startling in the purring elevator. "Love is for the birds," he said.

Bonnie glanced up at George and saw his thoughts were elsewhere. It pleased her that she was able to read his looks. He was anxious to get home. He was holding her hand. With a thrill she realized that it was to be with her. "Is it?" she said to Mr. Buffy.

"I'm not saying I wasn't in love," Mr. Buffy said in a low voice. He tipped his ear in their direction, but kept his back to them, with his hand on the elevator handle, doing his job. "Twenty years ago. But it doesn't last." Mr. Buffy shook his head. "Not that I don't love my wife," he went on, "but things change. You'll see. Things get different." He shrugged. "That's why it's for the birds."

Bonnie noticed that Mr. Buffy was not wearing his usual brass-buttoned uniform. It gave her a pang of worry for him. He was wearing a cardigan and crimson athletic pants. She figured he had not planned to be on duty tonight, and was filling in for the night doorman. She felt how fortunate she and George were. Except for classes, she could juggle her hours, and George did not appear to answer to anyone. No job would force either of them away from home on a cold night. George squeezed her hand and she looked up at his handsome profile, his boyish face. It was a face which seemed untouched. For one dizzy moment, Bonnie felt Mr. Buffy was far more real.

The elevator reached the lobby and she and George stepped out hand in hand. Mr. Buffy followed them across the black-and-white floor, hands deep in his pockets, head lowered. "Isabel," Mr. Buffy said philosophically, "she used to be in love."

Bonnie said, "Oh, but she is again."

"Sure, sure," said Mr. Buffy. "Every week, every month, every hour, Isabel's in love." Bonnie smiled. Mr. Buffy was right. Isabel would end up examining her boyfriends with an eye to their attributes and inevitably they didn't measure up. This one drank too much, this one had no sense of humor, another was not interested enough in sex. That was the wonderful thing about Bonnie's love for George so far—it didn't have to do with characteristics or personality. She loved him wholeheartedly, no questions asked.

Mr. Buffy stood in front of the glass door with the iron leaf grillwork behind and held the doorknob. But he didn't turn it; he was keeping them there. "That's why it's for the birds," he said. It seemed as if no one wanted them to leave tonight. Bonnie found a sort of comfort in it. It made her feel warm. George was not responding in the same way.

"Well, we'll wait and see," he said tersely.

"But you enjoy it," said Mr. Buffy, speaking in a low voice to Bonnie, who was, at least, receptive. "While you can." The door slowly opened.

The night air was cold and sharp. "We will," she said. George's hand was at the small of her back, urging her forward. She let herself be pushed by the force of the hand, and sank back against the authority of it, but the worry had appeared again, making her slightly uneasy. "Night," she called back to Mr. Buffy.

Bonnie and George headed off on the sidewalk.

"Because—" they heard. It was Mr. Buffy calling after them. Bonnie turned, craning her neck over George's leather shoulder. Mr. Buffy was standing in the freezing cold in his cardigan sweater with one arm raised underneath the stark light of the awning's bulb. He had come out after them with something more to say. But Bonnie would never know what it was: George whisked her around the corner.

Everything lately was going fast. It was like being in a wave. Normally she'd still be upstairs chatting with Isabel over coffee, taking in the rosy afterglow of dinner. She was, she had to admit, behind at work. A stack of papers she'd put on her desk had, after a couple of days, begun to look permanent, and it was harder to think about moving it. Other things that had mattered a great deal to her a month ago she could hardly recall—it was as if they had become weightless objects and were drifting about in a gravity-free air, no longer of concern to her. Instead, substantial before her was George's untroubled face.

They stood on Madison and looked down the empty avenue at the lights sparkling way downtown. Not a cab in sight. George pivoted. "Let's go over to Fifth," he said and strode off on long legs. It was like being in a race. Bonnie wanted to cry out, What's the rush? The other night they'd gone out to a movie with her brother and George had not wanted to get a drink afterward. They had hurried home. Then when they got there, George had turned on the TV. Bonnie asked him if there was something he wanted to see and he said, Not really, he just wanted to let his mind wander, just wanted to stop thinking for the day. He had held his arms out to her and said, Come here, and she'd nestled in his arms while he changed the channel with the automatic device, not having to move. Bonnie thought of that now, of his not having to move and not wanting to think.

"What's the matter, baby?" said George, his voice sweet. "Why the dragging feet?"

His arm came back and went around her. "Nothing," she said. Though it was minor, she was aware of it being her first lie to him.

·

Later at home—they went back to Bonnie's tiny apartment—Bonnie asked him how work was that day and he said, Fine, with a clipped tone, meaning he did not want to talk about it. But now Bonnie was irritated he'd taken her early from Isabel's.

"But what did you do?" she said. He was on the bed with a book. "Something interesting? Any detail will do."

George, head against a pillow, kept his eyes on his book. "It was a day at work," he said. "No big deal."

"I know." Bonnie kicked off her boots. "I was just wondering what you do. I realize I don't really know."

"Nothing interesting," he said. "Believe me. If it were interesting I'd tell you."

"But I like to know how it's not interesting," she said, trying to sound encouraging. She sat next to him.

"Well, it's boring. I had a boring day at work. I discussed some idiotic ideas with idiots." He looked across his shoulder at her. "Satisfied?"

It was one of those questions one doesn't want an answer to. She shifted away from him.

"Where are you going?" he cried.

"To get ready for bed."

"Come back soon," he said, smiling. The face meant to soften her, but she turned away from it and tried to think of something else. She'd been in a lovely slow dream and did not want it to end. But once a person became aware of being in a dream it was difficult to stay asleep. The thing that kept one asleep was not knowing that you were sleeping, and not thinking. She tried to block out any further disturbance, but a voice came, insistent, breaking through the dream membrane. Hurry, the voice said, getting louder, Hurry.

· CAFÉ MORT ·

It's always an endless night. I come in when it's light outside and at some point, which I never see because I'm setting up or seeing to the few stray people who come in here early, night falls and before I know it the floor-to-ceiling windows on the café side are black. Car headlights pass in the darkness and you can see the bullet shapes of people's heads blotting out blurry lights as they move up and down the street, so it's not complete darkness.

Jerry our manager stands at the door between eight and ten, otherwise he lets Sharon do the seating, even though he's still on. He lost his brother in the Gulf War and wears an army pin on his lapel. Jerry is a jerk and I avoid him as much as I can, but if you want to keep your job you have to get along with people.

It is only out of desperation a person would take this job, waiting on dead people. Some of the waitresses are proud of it. Not me. But a person has to work. I don't register myself unless I think and gather my thoughts for at least a minute, and that's impossible in this place. It's the story with work, turns out; it

keeps you from thinking. Instead you are occupied with fascinating details like which person wants onions on her coffin or how
many more pieces of Daisy Pie are left in the fridge or which order
got switched back from the Terminal Tortellini to the Cremated
Shrimp.

The usual girls are on tonight. Sharon has a well made-up
face, with coral lipstick, and looks more like a banker than a wait-
ress. She takes great care with her tables, holding the pepper
grinder out stiffly in front of her. Rita is long-legged and wants
to be an actress. She brings in yogurt for supper, is on a diet, and
admits to being always hungry. Her bangs sprout in a soft wave
over her forehead. When she swings around a corner her ponytail
fans out leaving a bird shadow on the parquet floor, the only nice
thing about this place. The men at the bar watch her with longing
and resentment.

Then there's Karen who's been here forever. Grief has made
her gray around the eyes, as if someone pressed a dirty sponge
to them. She slips into the bathroom hallway and smokes Silva
Thins, taking quick, intense drags, four in a row, before hurrying
back when the cook screams that an order is up.

•

When I got to work tonight I felt something strange. Maybe
my patience is running out, I thought. I felt at the end of my rope.
I admit I've felt that before but usually at the end of a shift, and
then at night I go home and take a hot bath and lie in the tub
on my stomach, rocking the water and imagining I'm on a boat.
None of us can get to sleep right away. Sharon has a bowl of pop-

corn and watches TV to calm down. Rita smokes a joint. Then before you know it the next day has come and you're here again. It's difficult to get out of a rut.

But something is going on tonight. I have a different feeling. Even Jerry notices. As I'm putting the ugly topaz candle jars on the tables, he says, "Hey"—still not knowing my name even though I've been here awhile—"with your hair back like that you look sort of cute," surprised. I've been wearing my hair the same the whole time. Then he goes back to knocking his fists together, waiting for the night to get busy.

I suddenly think, What if this were the last night I was here? The thought is newly alluring. But I don't get carried away with it, believe me.

•

Gil, a regular, is in his usual place hunched at the bar with his baseball cap on. "Turn off that shit," he's saying. On the TV is a baby being born. You learn about regulars pretty fast by osmosis. Gil was shot in a hunting accident. A few stools down is Manny in his spot. "You better shut up or I'll turn *you* off," he says. Manny, a big guy, no surprise had a heart attack.

Mac is the bartender—he and his girlfriend used to hang glide. Being an employee, he was the survivor. He specializes in insults. "I'm just trying to bring a little light and laughter into this hole," he says. When Jerry's back is turned, he flicks bottle caps at the hanging crepe lampshade which hovers over his dark, bottomless floor back there.

There are three girls in a row at the bar with their legs crossed, rib cages tilted up. They laugh together, each with a different look for Mac. The first one lowers her eyes, clamping her lips around her cocktail straw. The one in the middle, the boldest, talks for everyone. The third, shy, is folding her square napkin, having finished her drink first, and ordering another. Someone said she was the one driving when they crossed the median into oncoming traffic.

Some customers are okay. There's a nice man with cropped silver hair and coffee-colored skin who comes in on Thursdays. He's polite. From where I stand politeness counts for a lot.

"We'd like the Grilled Shovels and the house red," he says. "But no fries, please. We're watching our weight." He looks up. "We're saving it for dessert." He always dines alone. We found out he's a twin, but his brother's still alive. After I take his order, he says, "We thank you," and goes back to his book.

Roman and Neil are here tonight. They keep to themselves, trade their soups halfway through. Roman was on an airplane which went down, headed for Fort Lauderdale, and Neil had cancer already, but drank ammonia to join Roman. They smoke like chimney stacks and talk in a steady stream to each other in low close voices. The theme here is devotion. Though as we waitresses know, devotion can keep a person locked in, too. Everyone who works here has that in common. We're all stuck in the irons of devotion. Sharon nursed her dad over a long illness till he went. Rita still wears the leather jacket of her boyfriend who wiped out in it. Just now she dropped the blue-cheese dressing container and our station is like a white rink. There's a new girl shadowing her tonight, Maggie, who stands by, haunted. She looks the way I did when I started; I think I've actually changed. I'm betting she's an orphan.

I have my qualifier, too, though I don't talk about him. He was young, my beloved. An outdoors man. A crevasse in Alaska is all you need to know.

•

"Marry a man," says Gil, holding up a small pitchfork with an olive on it, "who fascinates you."

The regulars seem to come in for the sole purpose of handing out advice. Clichés abound.

"Never tell the whole story," they say.

"Keep your family close."

"You can only trust your mother."

At the bar it never stops. "You only go around once" . . . "Life's worth living" . . . "You do what you gotta do" . . . "You can't take it with you" . . . "What're you waiting for?" etc. Coming from these people you can see it as either instructive or ironic, depending on your perspective.

I ask the Chinese cooks in the kitchen, What year is it? The Year of the Dog. Sharon, who studied religion and the Far East, says, whispering, that the dog guards people in the afterlife. The head cook, Ring—though I think it's really Ling, but everyone calls him Ring—lost his nephew at sea.

Tonight the cooks are pouting and seem particularly disappointed. Have I not noticed that before? They're listening to the radio in their language. At the end of the night they'll make noodles and crab and egg cakes for supper, their own cuisine, and it smells like the docks back there.

•

The guy with eyes ringed like a raccoon's is dining on the shredded pencil: I figure a writer.

"More coffee?" I ask him.

"No," he grumbles. "It wasn't fresh *and* it was putrid."

Karen says he used to be a priest, but left the priesthood.

"It didn't answer all the questions," he explained.

The beige woman is in tonight. She has beige hair, a beige suit, and beige panty hose. Her bag is also beige. She sits alone, but she likes to have the table for four in the corner so she can face out to the room. She says she doesn't like anyone behind her. Sometimes she buys drinks for the bankers. She hardly looks up, just watches the miniature TV she carries in her purse. She asks me if we have diet Scrambled Clouds.

"Scrambled Clouds are diet," I say.

She orders them and eats one bite. When I put down her bill she looks up from the TV. "The point of life is love," she says wide-eyed, apparently having just discovered it. Karen says she was a suicide.

Everyone has his or her attitude.

The tiny woman with her hair pulled back tight is a Russian dancer. She orders the same whenever she comes in, September Odes. Sharon says her dances were famous for expressing despair: people running endlessly in place or staring out at the audience with accusing expressions. Or, her dancers would just stand, mouths open in silent screams. Once, going by, I heard her say to Sharon, "Happy? What the hell is there to be happy about?"

If you divide people into those who look at the positive side of life and those who see things more generally in the negative department, then I'd say there's a good cross section of humanity here. Some people feel they've suffered more than others; others feel lucky and fortunate. Pretty much across the board, the people's lives, at least what we can see of them from our point of view, are filled with the same amount of pain and suffering and good fortune and bad, but some handle it more gracefully than others. One might say that the lucky ones are the people who feel they're lucky.

Rita is counting a tip. "Divide this four ways and you got bus fare to nowhere," she says.

•

Frankly I don't notice much difference between the people in here and the ones who don't come in, but I suppose that's why I have this job.

Purple Fingers waves me over. "Excuse me, miss." I look at her. I'm tired and I look. She is wearing a scarf of lilacs. "I'm being bitten to death by mosquitoes," she says. "Ever since I walked in here." She scratches her thigh as proof. Some customers come in just to complain. I tell her I'll mention it to the manager. Then she looks at the dessert menu.

"What'll I have?" she says. "I can't decide."

"Have the fattening thing," says the larger woman with her. She's wearing a gold noose necklace. "And I'll stay thin."

The new girl, Maggie, is at the counter waiting for some beers. I hear her say she lost her parents in a diving accident. I feel proud that I spotted it.

•

The electrocuted woman who comes in occasionally tonight brings her little girl with her. The kid smashes a coffee cup and dumps all the sugar packets into her lap. Her mother doesn't notice a thing. When the daughter sweeps the menu rack off the table, it clatters to the floor and everyone ignores it, not wanting to embarrass the electrocuted woman for some reason. Some deaths receive extra reverence. Karen deals with it, picking it up and saying, No problem, having more patience than all of us. Karen's little brother fell out of an apartment window when Karen was five. She had dared him to touch a pigeon. Some things are harder to live with than others.

Jerry seats a family of three at a center table. They want only dessert. For drinks the parents order coffee and the little boy says, "I'd like a queen-sized tea," which makes them all laugh. They drowned in a sailing accident and everyone looks happy. They order Morphine Supremes with vanilla ice cream.

The thing about going in an accident is that a person exits his life unaware of his departure. An old-timer might see departure on the horizon. Does it matter much?

One judge who comes tottering in some nights left the bench when he was ninety-eight. He says his life was long because he didn't get angry at people and didn't fret about things he couldn't control. "That'll kill you," he says.

There's a Mr. Putnam who comes in. He's blind. He tried to commit suicide when he was twenty but instead blinded himself and says afterward, he felt grateful for the rest of his life. The woman with the braids on her head who was an archaeologist says the secret to life is to keep walking through it without analyzing it too much or clinging to it too much. Just to keep walking. That was my beloved's attitude, but look where it got him.

Gil is being his usual jerk. "Can I wipe the ashes off your apron?" he says to Rita as she walks by.

"The tonic in this drink tastes funny," Manny says.

"So laugh," says Rita over her shoulder. Maggie follows behind, learning fast. You can see this beginning to suit her. You can see her relief at finding this job.

•

The night wears on. Bitterness, anger, and recrimination are the prevailing themes among the late-night clientele. No one's eating anymore, just drinking. "I never got a chance," says the woman at the end of the bar to no one, smoking a pipe. Everyone starts to lose it.

Mac washes glasses and leaves them upended. "Jerry, you interested in the numbers?" he says.

Jerry is standing at the door. "Stick with your work, Mac," Jerry says, keeping his back to the bar.

Then a group comes in. It's unusual for anyone to come in this late. It's a woman in a white nightgown with a paramedic on either side of her. The paramedics in white pants and shirts were driving an ambulance which got broadsided by some idiot at a red light. The woman in the nightgown looks bewildered. The paramedics immediately abandon her to sit at the bar. They order White Russians and split a bowl of Elegies, leaving their patient unattended.

The woman in the nightgown is probably in her seventies. She's wearing a soft light blue sweater over her nightgown, and has an IV pole wheeling along beside her. Her hair is nicely done; still, she looks frail. Jerry doesn't seem to know what to do with her and points her to a stool farther down the bar. The woman moves away from him dismissively.

Sharon breezes by me. "Two Floods on seven," she says, barely moving her lips, face polished as porcelain. I get the Floods and deliver them, and coming back I pass the nightgown woman half perched on a barstool, facing out. Her eye catches mine. She has a strong, direct gaze. Sometimes you see truth in a face. This woman looks flabbergasted; I see she's right. She's not in my section, but then she's not in anyone's section and Mac is behind her, wiping his hands, chatting up the paramedics. I stop and ask the woman if there's anything I can get her.

"Excuse me," she says. She has a nice rich voice.

"Yes?"

She shakes her head. "I don't belong here," she says. She smirks, perfectly willing to forgive the mistake.

"You don't?" I say.

"No," she says and lifts her arm as if to say, See? Need I say more?

Alongside the IV, she is emaciated and despite her coiffure does look very sick.

"I'm not gone yet." This is apparently comic to her. "There's been a mistake."

"It's okay," I say. I'm saying what everyone always says. But this woman calls me on it.

"No, it's not okay." Her face is defiant. She jerks her head in the direction of her minders down the bar. One is laughing open-mouthed at Mac. "You sound like them."

She holds my gaze and I'm surprised to see her eyes clear as paperweights, with tiny angles of light in the blue. I would have expected rheumatic, sick eyes. Someone looks at you hard that way, it gives you agita, but in a good way.

"Well, it's not forever," I say, grasping at straws. She has unnerved me.

"Don't you believe it," she says. Her bony hand comes out and latches on to my arm.

We're fused together for a moment and I feel oddly calm.

Out of nowhere a laughing paramedic appears behind her and takes her firmly at her shoulder. "Come on, Anita," she says, steering her. "Come sit with us."

The woman gets off the stool and goes where she is taken but looks over her shoulder at me. "You don't belong here either," she says.

People say things that have a physical effect. It must be particular to humans that words can do that. That woman's words hit me and reverberate like a tolling bell through my body.

The paramedic has dragged her over to where they sit at the bar, but I see the woman's mind is elsewhere, not listening to their banter. I start collecting the salt and pepper from the tables and the next time I look over all three of them are gone.

The smoking woman is still there, emptying her pipe. "Happy Obituary," she cries to no one in particular. No one looks. That's an old one. Minutes later she's asleep on her arms.

At the station I refill the coffee which has dried into a syrup at the bottom of the beaker. I toss out the old grounds and get a premeasured packet and when I rip the metal paper the coffee grounds fly everywhere. Luckily we're not busy so I don't have to hurry to get the dust brush and sweep it up. Then I make another pot. As the water is gurgling down I am struck by something. In the past five minutes I have not thought of my beloved at all. It's a sort of record. He's usually there in my head, like a shadow in front of every thought. I feel guilty. Then I realize the reason I wasn't thinking of him was because I was thinking of someone else for a change, of the woman in the nightgown. I was thinking about her saying I didn't belong here. Maybe I don't.

Now, thinking about my beloved again, I see his back. His back and shoulders are very characteristic parts of him. Suddenly I feel how absorbing it has been to think of him all the time, even when I chose it. The woman in the nightgown made me wonder for a change about what she was going through. She seemed to be doing the same about me. That's a new open feeling. A patch of warmth spreads below my collarbones, surprising me. I didn't know I had even been cold.

At the end of the night the last thing we do is make sure things are stocked or cleaned and ready for the next day. We fill the saltshakers, etc. I've noticed that when I'm doing things close-up with my hands, my mind reflects back to me, less distracted by what's around it. I'm filling up a saltshaker and he, my beloved, appears. He's usually there when I do something close-up. Only this time salt is pouring over his face and he wavers in and out of focus, as if being erased by snow in a blizzard. Then he disappears altogether.

The air becomes—how can I describe it?—softer. Sounds turn gentle and the people and the tables and the bar and the lights recede. I feel more of myself and yet don't feel in place. Sharon passes me with an intent look. I notice Mac staring at a little section of mirror between the bottles. Everyone seems to be moving each in his or her own column. I see Maggie, concentrating at the cash register. She's dug in now.

I see how everyone is enveloped in an individual daze. But I am cracked out of it. I feel clear. It's as if they are all floating. But I'm not with them in the column. I'm unencased.

My arms feel weirdly strong, with that feeling of being outside in the summer, full of nature and invigorated, not worried about anything or even wanting anything. Though the feeling actually gives you a hunger. Your body is in fine working order. It feels restless and happy and would like to run or lift something up or swim underwater or dance or take up with another body, one with a pulse, one that can move and stay close and be warm and alive.

"Hel-*lo*," Rita says, bunching forks and knives in the silverware tray. "Where are you?" She hovers near me, indistinct. "Have we lost you?"

Losing someone is the last thing I want to think about now.

"I'm here," I say. "I'm here."

But part of me has already left. I'm out the door.

Much later, it was the trees he would think of.

They had been so tall and bare. He would have seen them when he'd first gone to the Boston Common when he was eight years old, but he didn't remember then noticing the trees. Now, when he thought of that day in December, he would see the spaced-apart oaks with their spidery branches, reaching into the stark afternoon, leafless black skeletons, towering above him. But oddly he would picture them from above, looking down through their branches to his fifteen-year-old self, beside the melting snow-banks and the other people teetering around on the park paths.

•

Hockey practice had let out early that day at St. Peter's when their coach's wife finally went into labor. The boys were all laughing at how freaked Mr. D looked, forgetting to take the goals off the ice, and had given him shit when he had left for the hospital and had to go deal with it.

So Ned had taken a train earlier than usual out of the dinky train station in Concord. It was a quiet time of afternoon and no one else was boarding the squeaking car, except for an old lady in a light blue coat who was so curled over she could barely make it up the stairs. Watching her deliberate progress beside the conductor, Ned thought how bad that would be, to be so old you'd basically have to stare down the whole time.

It was Christmas vacation, but Ned hadn't been able to go home yet; the hockey team still had a few days' practice. The dorms were closed, and most of the other boarders on the team were staying with day students in Concord, but Ned was staying with his aunt Elsie, who lived in Cambridge near Harvard Square.

To get there he had to take the train to Boston and then the subway to Cambridge, but once he got to the big house on Craigie Street the food was tasty. His father was making him stay there because of everything going on at home. Normally they didn't see Aunt Elsie, his father's sister, because she was considered an oddball in the family. But now his dad needed her help. Aunt Elsie was actually pretty nice, Ned thought, and fed him giant meals and maybe appreciated having another person at the table since Uncle Rob hardly said a word, not that Ned did either, but at least she had another person to listen to her. She had a lot of opinions about Reagan winning and how bad it was for the country and about the hostage crisis. Ned had figured it was better than staying at Mike O'Conner's house, where he'd been assigned. Word was the O'Conners had the TV ban. That night *M*A*S*H* would be on, and he had his own TV at Aunt Elsie's. He could watch whatever he wanted. He even watched *The Waltons*, which he actually liked though he didn't admit it to anyone. On *The Waltons* everybody actually cared about one another.

When he got off the train at North Station it was practically deserted. Where was everybody today? He walked out from the shaded tracks into the station with its polished ocher floor. Ned was tall for fifteen and thin, with brown corduroy pants slipping off his hips. He wore a plaid shirt and work boots with the laces undone. His navy-blue parka, unzipped, had an L-shaped patch of hockey tape in the front from when Zeigler pushed him into the iron arrows on the chapel railing and ripped it.

Since he had extra time, instead of taking the subway to Cambridge as he had every other stupid day, he decided he'd go walk around. He vaguely knew the Boston Common was nearby.

He trudged up the hill toward downtown, past shops jammed with crap tied in ribbons and colored lights shaped like bullets and streetlights wound with fake ivy. It was weirdly warm. You could see your breath in the shade, but when you crossed the street, the sidewalk gutters were gushing with water and you could feel the sunshine. Sooty mounds of snow along the sidewalk were eroded into peaks. People went by holding square paper bags with red trim or briefcases or kids' hands. His hands were in his pockets, hunkered down. He had his wallet in one. It was an old one that his dad had given him when he'd gotten a new one.

He got to the top of the hill where Government Center spread out as a brick-paved arena with levels and handrailings. He knew the Common was somewhere close and turned down a few streets narrow as canyons till he miraculously saw at the end of one crisscrossing tree branches and brown-and-white earth. Here, he'd heard, he could supposedly find someone to sell him pot.

It had been spring when he'd been there before seven years ago, with his mother and older brother, Matt. They'd come to go to the Swan Boats, and were dressed in their Boston clothes, gray flannel shorts with suspenders underneath their sweaters. Matt's sweater was dark blue and Ned's dark green; otherwise they were dressed exactly the same. Ned couldn't believe they'd worn those things. Ned had never been into the city before just to walk around. The Baldwins used to drive through the city along the Charles River on their way to Brookline to visit their grandparents or, once, after the Ice Capades, they drove along the perimeter of the park to see the gold dome on the State House, and their mother pointed out the brick building where she'd first met their father at a party.

At the Swan Boats Ned remembered they'd gotten red-and-white cardboard boxes of popcorn and had thrown kernels to the swans and ducks while a man at the front of the boat pedaled what looked like steps. The boats weren't really swans the way Ned had imagined them; they just had wooden cutouts on the sides in the shape of swan silhouettes with wing-tipped tails. Otherwise they were normal boats with red benches. Still, he'd felt it had been cool to be in Boston. The three of them went to Schrafft's for lunch and had sundaes for dessert. His mom was dressed up, too, in a dark pink dress with a matching jacket, and her pearls. She was happy watching Matt eat his hot fudge and Ned his butterscotch and stole bites with her spoon. His mother liked treats, but was trying to keep her figure. That was one thing about their mother, she knew what it was like to be a kid. She didn't try to make them into adults, the way Dad tried, correcting the way you talked, or telling you how you were doing something wrong. It was something he'd liked about his mom then, that she was more like a kid, but now, getting older, he sort of wished she were more like a grown-up.

It was weird being in the city alone. He stood under the amazingly tall trees near a trash can and unwrapped a Snickers. A woman loitered nearby. She had slicked hair parted in the middle and rounded into a ball at her neck. She wore a rust-colored leather jacket belted at the waist and narrow blue jeans with a flair. Her sunglasses were tinted brown, darker at the top. Each cheek was smudged with a brownish rouge. Sienna, he thought, knowing the color from his oil-painting art class.

The woman walked by Ned, not meeting his eye. "Pot?" she whispered, holding her lapel with crimson fingernails.

Ned looked around. There was a businessman in a suit moving briskly toward the subway. Three ladies, probably secretaries, walked beside one another in skirts and snow boots. An old woman had a net over her hair. No one was paying them the slightest bit of attention. "Okay," he said.

The woman nodded, still not looking him in the eye. Ned couldn't believe how easy this was.

It was definitely going to blow away Matt when he got home and they went down to the rocks after dinner and Ned brought out the pot. So far it was either Matt or their neighbor Barney who had supplied it. At school Ned had heard Sander Lawrence say there were guys selling it all over the Common. Sander had gotten his from a hippie at Thanksgiving, he said, passing a joint with both nonchalance and reverence to Ned and his best friend, Zeigler, huddled behind the maintenance shed as the white sunset shot through the pine trees during the two minutes they had before needing to be at the refectory for dinner.

The woman gestured with her head. She turned, and Ned followed her, looking down to the square heels of her boots. A car went by blasting music, *Another one bites the dust* . . . The woman's shoulders went forward and back, forward and back, like someone exaggerating. Ned had seventeen dollars on him—he figured he could borrow more later from Aunt Elsie if he needed it, which he probably would for the train home tomorrow after the last practice. The subway to Cambridge was seventy-five cents. He would set that aside. If the pot were more, he'd just ask the lady for half. He would bargain, make a deal.

The woman headed into the subway entrance and started down the stairs. Ned kept a few feet behind her. Then she stopped in the echoing underpass and leaned against the blue-and-white-tile wall, facing away from him. Ned hesitated, expecting another signal. Should he go over there? The woman looked over her shoulder, pursing her lips.

He had that nervous feeling he got at the beginning of a game, or before seeing a teacher during office hours, that something uncertain was going to happen and he would be blamed for whatever it was, whether or not it was something he'd actually done. He thought of how Matt did things with natural assurance, as if it were obvious. Ned walked over and stood next to the woman, his hands in his pockets. She was tall, taller than he was.

"It's at my place," she said in a hoarse voice, matter-of-factly. She looked him up and down. "You'll have to come there."

Close-up Ned saw that her skin was covered with thick foundation and powder, which made it look bumpy. Around her neck was a thin green scarf. It was a thick neck. He felt something hot and terrible rush through him.

"Sorry," he said. He dropped his head a little and frowned to show he wanted to, but really couldn't. "I can't. I have to get to—"

The woman grabbed his arm. She had a hard grip. "I don't think so," she said. "I think you can come with me." Ned looked down and saw a small knife an inch from his dangling parka zipper. "It won't take long, sugar. Just to Charlestown."

Ned looked down at her hand gripping his arm. There were a lot of rings on the fingers. He saw some teal-green stones and black hairs sprouting below the knuckles. Out of the corner of his eye he felt figures walking by, but was too scared to look at them for help.

"Come on," she said and locked her arm in his arm. "Let's be nice."

Ned dragged his feet, but she was strong and heaved him along. She paid for him at the ticket booth, keeping her arm tight against his. She'd put the knife in one of her wide pockets but kept it pointing in Ned's direction.

She let him go through the turnstile before her. The platform had a lot of people on it; it was on the verge of rush hour. He thought, I could run. Should I run? Where would I go? This person is big. What if she caught me? She'd stab me. She'd only have to stab me a few times and I'd definitely die.

The subway car arrived with a screech and the woman kept her torso right up close to him as they stepped on, crowding in with everyone else. Ned looked around at the faces, on the low-key, searching for someone he could cry out to, who would protect him. But no one returned his gaze. He spotted a large black man hanging on to the bar, facing the opposite direction. That guy could nail this lady, he thought. When someone jostled him, the man turned his head and looked straight at Ned, but through him, with no interest whatsoever.

In his ear he heard, "Last thing I want to do is hurt you. So stop worrying. Everything will be fine."

•

A woman holding a shopping bag on her lap glanced up at them, sizing them up as a couple with a disapproving face. Ned wanted desperately to explain and realized how crazy it was that he cared about what some stranger on the subway thought when he had a knife pointing at his stomach. It was an old train; it rattled and chugged. Then it stopped. Everyone sat silently in the tunnel. He couldn't try to run here. He just had to wait. Then the train crept forward with a piercing screech at the turn. Ned covered an ear and stared at what little he could see through the window opaque with dirt. When the train came up from underground the sun was gone and the sky streaked with wisps of gray smog.

Forty miles north was his hometown, Marshport. It had a harbor and three different churches, the most prominent of which was a classic New England church right smack in the middle of the town green. Its steeple had been the focus of a recent fundraising drive—wood rot was threatening its structure and safety required it be removed—and everywhere you went in town there were little clear plastic boxes with SAVE THE STEEPLE signs, stuffed with coins and dollar bills. His mother, who despite attending the Catholic church, where she dragged Ned and Matt for as long as she could before they were old enough simply to refuse to go, had taken up the cause. For some reason Ned thought of his hometown then and with longing of the steeple.

At the Charlestown stop, the doors opened and the woman, with a determined but calm face, urged him onto the platform. There were fewer people here as they walked up the stairs, and Ned was struck by how normal everyone around him seemed. They were all heading home or going to work or doing something that wasn't full of fear or desperation. He wished with all his might that he were like them again.

The woman didn't say anything as they walked along a street lined with small houses behind chain-link fences. He thought, Maybe she just wants to make sure I pay for the pot. He wasn't sure what was going on, but he was terrified regardless. A knife in her pocket.

At the corner, Ned saw a small grocery and was relieved when they got up to it and the woman sort of steered him to enter.

"Pack of Trues," said a big man in front of them at the bodega. Going into a store was reassuring to Ned. This woman wasn't so desperate that she wasn't doing normal things. The man behind the counter looked over the shoulder of the True man.

"*Cómo estás?*" he said to the woman with Ned and reached back to the cigarettes.

"*Dos, por favor,*" the woman said. Two packs of Parliaments stacked on top of each other were placed on the counter. "Matches too." Now Ned heard she had a slight accent, but he had no idea what it was.

Ned tried to catch the eye of the man behind the counter, a guy in his fifties or sixties with a low, dark hairline, but he had the sort of face that had been set like a mask years ago with creases in the forehead and a mouth pressed tight. It didn't look as if his gaze wanted to take in anything new.

This lady was probably always bringing young boys back to her place to score. What did the man behind the counter care?

•

Six months earlier Ned's father had left Ned's mother because he was now in love with a woman he'd met in Chicago on a business trip the previous spring. He had sat next to her on the bus while they were touring a plant he was visiting. She was a businessperson like him, a little younger than their mother, he'd conceded to his sons when he explained it all to them that July. Her name was Mary Ellen, he said, and they had fallen in love with each other and she very much wanted to meet the boys. Ned's mother was not in the room for this information. Ned and Matt supposed she'd heard it already, or else their father wouldn't have dared tell them. She was out at the Rentschlers' for cocktails. It was a golden summer evening, a Friday at their summer house on the Cape. Mr. Baldwin had just arrived. There'd been thunderstorms all day and now the air was clear and freshly cold.

"So you're divorcing Mum?" Matt had said.

"Your mother and I have been growing apart for some time," said Ned's father. He was leaning forward on the wicker sofa, elbows on knees, clapping his hands together slowly and silently.

"Where's Mary Ellen now?" Matt was always the one who knew what the important information to gather was. The answer was a surprise.

"She's nearby," their father said. To his credit, he looked pained. Ned could see he was trying to be straight with his kids. "She's at a hotel in Sandwich." It was the next town over.

Sandwich? Did that mean they were going to meet her now? "Does Mom know?" Matt asked. His eyes were low and unfeeling, not in the least being sympathetic to his dad.

"That she's here . . . no . . ."

"No, Dad. That you're divorcing her." Matt's head tilted back, his ear practically on his shoulder, and he was kind of snarling.

"Your mother understands everything going on," their father said, something Ned doubted very much. "But our main concern," he went on, "is how this will affect you two."

"Right," Matt spat under his breath.

"It hasn't been an easy decision, Matt. But I love Mary Ellen and there's nothing else for me to do. I don't have a choice."

"Actually, everyone has a choice." Matt had been studying debate in the spring, and Ned noticed a change in his tone of voice whenever he found an opportunity to practice it on the family. This was definitely the most substantial thing he'd come across yet. He sat up. "You can stay or you can go off with some other lady. There's always a choice."

Mr. Baldwin nodded slowly a few times, as if to concede he would take a few hits, he was willing to do that. His lips disappeared in his face. He looked at the wicker coffee table with the glass cover.

Matt turned sideways on his chair, away from his father. "You're lame, Dad," he said.

"What about you, Ned. Mad at your old man?"

Ned had taken off the bandanna he'd had around his head and was tying it tightly around his wrist. He didn't know what to say. So he expressed a worry. "So we're going to still live with Mom?"

"That's the idea." Mr. Baldwin sat up. "But I'll be seeing you a lot." He slapped his knees, meaning this must be over.

"Like when?" Ned said.

Mr. Baldwin stood up with a big smile. "Oh, all the time. All the time."

Matt didn't look at him; he wasn't going to give him the satisfaction of attention.

•

Since that Friday in July Ned had seen his dad three times. Their mother didn't allow their dad to come by. On a Saturday in September his father had taken Ned and Matt to the Harvard game. In November, at the start of Thanksgiving vacation, he'd driven Ned home from St. Peter's, dropped him off at their house, his father's previous house, then turned around and drove back to his apartment on Beacon Hill, where he was now living with Mary Ellen.

Later that night on the Cape after Mr. Baldwin had left, Ned and Matt went to their station behind the lattice divider of the porch, where the lights from the porch came through in check-

ered shadows, and passed a joint back and forth. Their mother
had stumbled up to bed after a fake cheerful good night in the
living room, clinking together a few bottles in the dining room on
her way, so they didn't talk that night about Mr. Baldwin's news.
His mother didn't like to talk about gloomy things. Ned was noting stonedly how the joint looked like a slightly oranger version
of the fireflies blinking at the edge of the lawn when suddenly
they heard from an upstairs window a few strange high intakes of
breath as if someone were suffocating. Both of them froze. It was
so fleeting that when it stopped they weren't sure it hadn't been
part of an insect chorus, or even music coming from the house
party next door.

•

Ned smelled burning garbage as he and the woman walked a
few slushy blocks down a quiet street to a beige house. A busted
front-door window was covered with cardboard, doing nothing to
keep out the sudden cold. The woman unlocked a padlock and
then put a key in the next door. Nobody knows where I am, Ned
thought. No one in the whole world. He thought, I could run now
and what if she ran after me and stabbed me in the street, I'd lie
there bleeding and die and if she took my wallet no one would
even know who I was.

"Up we go," the woman said and followed Ned in. They went
up three flights beside a thick railing, switching back to go up
each flight, and stopped at a door with a pale-blue pussycat decal
sparkling on it.

"Come on, baby. Be a good boy and I'll be nice." She said it with a soft tone and Ned tried to see this as a good sign. But the whole thing was not looking good at all, the whole thing was a bunch of bad signs.

She opened the door and flicked her hand for him to go in first. It was one room sort of divided by a couch with a kitchen on one side by a window and a bed against the wall on the other. The bed had a pink satin cover on it.

Covering the wall by the bed were framed pictures, all of the woman, studio shots of her dressed up in feathers, wearing hot pants, in a sequined dress with a top hat onstage in the spotlight, in cheesecake poses with her butt out and mouth pouting. She saw him looking at them. "I dance at Starlite down in the District. You should come see me sometime." Ned couldn't believe she was telling him where she worked. Didn't that mean that nothing bad could happen?

"You're pretty cute," she said, and pushed back the hair from Ned's forehead. It was weird, it was a thing his mother did. He felt a wave of nausea and thought, What's she going to do if I faint?

She sat on the bed and unzipped her boots. She patted the shimmering pink beside her. "Come here. Come sit with Crystal." Now she was even telling him her name.

"Listen, I'm sorry. I really have to go. I have to catch a train."

"No, baby. No. Not yet. Come here." And then in a sort of harder voice, suddenly impatient, "Take off your coat."

He didn't see anywhere to put it and dropped the coat on the floor. He sat down beside her. The room smelled of powdery perfume.

"What's your name?"

"Ned." As soon as he said it he realized he should have lied.

What was his problem? She'd never have known his name. He had a terrified, drifting feeling, as if something beyond him like the ocean were sweeping him forward and he was supposed to just go along with this current, not fight it. There were so many things in the world you couldn't do anything about; this was just another one.

She picked up a short roach from a black ashtray on a bed-side table beside a white cat lamp and lit it. "This should help," she said. "This is what you were after, isn't it?" She took a toke and handed it to Ned. He took a toke and held in the smoke and waited to feel something. It didn't take even the slightest edge off his terror.

"Neddy, that's cute." She put her hand with its rings and long crimson fingernails on his crotch. She took another drag from the joint. "And what have we here, Neddy?" Then the abrupt, low voice. "Take off your pants."

Ned's body seemed to lift a couple of feet off the bed and after that it was as if he were watching through a thick glass aquarium. He kept sitting there and she started to move him around, and pulled off his corduroys. She stood and took off her jeans and her flesh-colored stretchy underpants with an unnatural bulge. He was pushed facedown on the bed. He thought his lungs would explode. What was that? Her sharp fingernail . . . then an awful, familiar softness. "Shit," Crystal was muttering. "What the fuck." She fumbled around. Ned closed his eyes, which brought him back close into his body, so he quickly opened them and kept them open, looking over a chipped windowsill at some flat, dark rooftops and tilted gray roofs. He could see the Bunker Hill Monument at the very edge of the window. If he didn't die, he kept thinking, this would be over soon. If he did die, this would be the last thing he saw: a room he didn't know with a bedside table and a cat lamp on it. She was mumbling swear words and poking at him with her fingers, then fumbling again. He also thought, I will never tell this to anyone. He would never be able to explain how he had let this happen to himself. He felt a sharp pain.

How long it went on he couldn't have said. But it wasn't that quick.

•

Then she got off him. "Get out of here," she said and threw Ned his coat. She didn't look at him. He did everything not to look at her either as he grabbed his pants and his boots without bothering with his socks. His arms felt all weak.

He opened the door and she didn't stop him. His legs felt shaky but relieved as he hurried down the stairs and out of the house. He didn't look back. The next day he would have practically no memory of the subway ride that took him back to the Red Line and then to Cambridge. It was dark when he got to his aunt Elsie's, later than usual. Aunt Elsie remarked on his ashen complexion. "They are working you too hard out on the ice," she said. "Come on. You need to eat." Ned said he wasn't feeling well and after hanging up his parka beside the other winter coats where they were luxuriously loaded deep in the hall closet he went upstairs and lay down on his bed in the guest room. He slept through till morning.

•

The third time he'd seen his father was at a dinner arranged so he and Matt could meet Mary Ellen. Across from the Marshport church with the rotting steeple was the Brown Mug, a restaurant the Baldwins knew only from driving by. It was here Ned's father chose to introduce his sons to the person he was in love with, at dinner one October evening. There was no natural light inside the Brown Mug; their father and Matt and Ned were led to a banquette. Mary Ellen was there already and she stood. She wore a ruffled white shirt and a dark skirt with a matching jacket, a suit, not like anything their mother would ever wear. Their mom wore things like purple Marimekko shirtdresses and pink lipstick and carried a handbag that she said came from France, made of quilted flowered fabric. Mary Ellen had a black purse with a snap top. Her hair was pulled back tight and piled on the top of her head, like a country-western singer's. She wasn't close to being as pretty as their mother. It would have been one thing if their dad had found, in his words, a dish, but Mary Ellen didn't fall into the category at all. Her actual face sort of looked like a man's.

Mary Ellen sat next to their father in the banquette. At dinner they didn't talk about anything. The candle on their table was a topaz tulip shape with mottled indentations as if fingertips had molded the liquid glass. Ned spent much of the dinner looking at the candle.

·

Ned waited a few weeks before he told Matt what had happened at the Boston Common. It was Presidents' Day, so they were both home for the weekend. Matt went to a different boarding school, Westminster, because their dad thought that, as brothers, they should carve out places of their own. Mrs. Baldwin had been checked into a rehab place in western Massachusetts for a couple of weeks, after their cleaning lady, Marsha, found her passed out in the basement in their dad's workshop. Luckily it had been one of Marsha's cleaning days. Their mom's friend Dionne Hayden had driven her to Silver Lane—Mrs. Hayden was very organized and cheerful and even knew the place because Mr. Hayden had been in and out a few times, and Matt and Ned were going to visit her the next day. They'd come home to get the car. Marsha picked them up at the bus station and drove them home. She was a soft-edged person with sympathetic eyes and a tentative manner and Ned noticed, following her oversize alpaca sweater on the way to her car, how she was straining to strike the right note of concern, but it came across as frightened. Ned knew that, at home, Marsha had a "challenged" daughter, whom he'd seen once down the hall when he'd gone with his mother to drop off hand-me-downs. The daughter had been sitting on the floor ineffectually batting stuffed animals. At home Marsha drove them up the winding driveway and told them to call her if they needed anything and that she'd left groceries in the fridge.

They made hamburgers for supper and Ned's stomach was roiling. His digestion had been sort of screwed up for the past month or so.

Even though alone in the house, the brothers retreated to the rec room past the basement stairs where Matt hid his bong to smoke. That's when Ned told him what had happened.

Matt listened with an incredulous look and Ned was relieved that he didn't seem to find anything in Ned's behavior to criticize.

Matt shook his head, and kept on shaking it. This was the sickest thing he had ever heard. Then he got worked up.

"Shit, man, I'm going to kill the guy," Matt said, holding in his toke. Then he let it out. "You know where he lives. We could track him down. We even know where he works. We could easily turn him in."

Ned drew in the smoke, unable to answer. He still felt he'd been the one who had allowed it to happen, and no matter how you saw it, it would always be that way. For a long time he had kept going over in his mind the times he could have run or tried to grab the knife. Why didn't he? He was too completely petrified, that's why.

They both agreed there was no point in telling their mother.

"You just show me where that fucking guy lives," Matt said. Matt was bigger than Ned, and stronger. He could really whale on someone if he wanted to.

"I'm not sure I could really find it again," Ned lied.

"We could go to the place he works. I'm telling you, we should get the guy. He can't get away with that."

"But what if they find out I was trying to buy pot? That would be bad."

They both frowned, thinking. The smoke was doing its job of lightening Ned's head and he thought of their mother, whom they'd see tomorrow. He pictured her in a wicker chair in a sort of sunroom looking out over a lawn of snow, as he'd seen in a movie.

"Well, we've got to tell someone," Matt said.

They looked at each other, but neither could come up with a suitable person to tell.

•

The next afternoon they were sitting, stoned, with their mother in a wood-paneled room with high windows and mustard-colored curtains. In the room were many other people sitting around in armchairs with low tables, some doing a puzzle at a table. Half the people in the room were smoking. Mrs. Baldwin was wearing her blue-and-white-flowered bathrobe, and her hair was flatter to her head than usual. She kept smiling weakly, and her voice was weak, too. She told Ned he needed a haircut and pretended to have a commanding expression. Then her face sort of crumbled.

"I'm so sorry, boys," she said, and started crying. "Your mother is having a time of it." The boys nodded, and even Matt couldn't come up with much to say. Ned thought in a distant way of the Boston Common, of the spidery net of trees, and even more distantly of the apartment with the pink bedspread and what had happened there. He had half a feeling that it had happened to someone else, which was weird but a relief. Their mother asked them about this Mary Ellen, and her tone changed to nasty, which they were relieved by, so they could at least talk about that. "She looked like a country-western singer," Ned said and his mother laughed, then started crying again. Their father's name did not come up.

•

That was the first time they visited their mother in a dry-out place and it wouldn't be the last. There would be a number of places after Silver Lane. There would be a place with "Hill" in the name in Connecticut and finally a place in Arizona where neither of the boys visited but which proved to be a turning point to success. Not so long after that, roles reversed, and it was Mrs. Baldwin visiting Ned. Matt would not go; he was married with two kids by then, and besides, he said, he didn't want to go through all that again. So Mrs. Baldwin would be the one to sit with Ned, looking plump and calm, bringing him things he didn't need and didn't want, nodding at her son in an understanding way. She would believe she understood what he was going through, but Ned knew she could not and remained unconvinced that anyone else had the least idea of what it felt like to be him.

· LISTEN ·

—We were all so surprised.

    —You were surprised? I wasn't surprised.

    —Shocked.

    —It was surprising how unhappy.

    —No one saw.

    —No one could see.

    —No one wanted to see.

    —*They* saw.

    —Didn't really think about it.

    —So they were right.

    —Of course they were right.

    —They were wrong.

    —Who's they?

    —They were . . .

    —They are.

    —They were seeing what they weren't.

    —Feeling left.

    —Who're they?

—Wanted what everybody else . . .

—Left out.

—Who's everybody?

—There were reasons for it.

—Can't ignore the numbers.

—People want.

—The numbers say it all.

—People are hoping.

—What the numbers mean . . .

—It's tribal.

—What the rich . . .

—People always want something.

—What the poor . . .

—People always want something new.

—Want something more.

—People always.

—Which people?

—The uncounted.

—They can't really believe.

—The ignored.

—They won't.

—They try.

—Just ignore it.

—They know who they are.

—They're to blame.

—Who's the problem?

—They're corrupt.

—They're the future.

—We're the problem.

—Liar.

—They're what's happening now.

—They're the heart.

—They won't.

—Who're they?

—Who're we?

—They were never.

—They don't care.

—They're insane.

—Used to be great.

—Why can't they get along?

—Clueless.

—Trying our best.

—Feeling forgotten.

—Just symbols of hate.

—Doesn't work anymore.

—Symbol of hope?

—Used to be great.

—Not trying.

—Have to fix . . .

—Have no choice.

—Making it worse.

—Did our best.

—It's human behavior.

—Must do better.

—It's from having no choices.

—Too rich.

—Wrong of them.

—The poor.

—Can't handle it.

—Leaving.

—Never leaving.

—Must do something.

—*Time for a change!*

—Our complacency.

—Not mine.

—Doesn't work anymore.

—Time to act.

—Not theirs.

—Who're they?

—We'll show them.

—What they're saying is—

—No one heard.

—They are . . .

—What they want to say.

—What they couldn't say.

—What they're thinking.

—What are they thinking?

—They couldn't say.

—No one was listening.

—The rich always . . .

—Can't be helped.

—Human nature.

—Can't be changed.

—Must be saved.

—Must be changed.

—Weirder every day.

—It's unreal.

—What I heard—

—Did something else happen?

—Can't watch.

—Can't listen.

—How can they?

—Can't dismiss it.

—Can't blame.

—So surprising.

—More and more each day.

—Less each day.

—Have to leave.

—I'm never leaving.

—What can we do?

—I thought we were—

—What will they do?

—Isn't fair.

—We didn't know.

—Seen it all.

—What about the kids?

—It's never been.

—Truly insane.

—Lost his mind.

—Never had it.

—He was great.

—Never in my lifetime.

—Only the rich.

—Like it was before.

—Ninety-nine percent.

—Keep fighting.

—It's no different.

—How do you like your meat done?

—Can't listen anymore.

—What're they saying?

—Can't watch.

—Can't stop watching.

—How can people?

—Can't sleep.

—What do they want?

—Please hold.

—How can people not?

—Not again.

—Stop complaining.

—Feeling threatened.

—Can't take it.

—Did something else happen?

—You mean Charlottesville?

—No, since then.

—Is there anyone better?

—Sorry. I'm late.

—Somebody must be able to—

—Who?

—She couldn't.

—She could have.

—She didn't.

—He did.

—He heard them.

—He was great.

—I miss him already.

—They hated him.

—We loved him.

—They love him.

—He heard them.

—Can't believe this.

—Can't be happening.

—Had to happen!

—They've finally gotten what—

—Can't go on.

—Can't stand to listen.

—Can't bear to watch.

—Has to change.

—Message is clear.

—What's the message?

—They're insane.

—Who thinks that?

—Has to stop.

—Blame the rise on the—

—Feeling threatened.

—No one listening.

—Accept the differences.

—Deliberate strategy.

—I can't talk about it.

—No one listening.

—He heard.

—No one heard.

—They heard him.

—Which them? Which him?

—Across the aisle.

—This is how I like my meat.

—Great again.

—Really worried now.

—Like the world has never seen.

—Not the way I like it.

—Lies.

—Getting what they want.

—Human behavior.

—I don't eat anything with eyes.

—Hell yeah.

—Must ignore it.

—All lies.

—Has to change.

—Nothing new.

—Never before.

—Once again.

—Haven't a clue.

—Pay attention.

—This is where I work.

—Not anymore.

—I never did, before . . .

—Can't stand it.

—Have to for my family.

—Still can't believe it.

—Can't imagine.

—Can't bear it.

—Can't look.

—Can't take another word.

—Are you listening?

wooden table, scraping their chairs. Sophie did retain over the years the impression of the professor sort of ignoring a male student attempting to say goodbye to him and instead calling to her as she reached the door.

Miss Vincent, he had said. Please wait. He had something to ask her. And she'd waited by the exit, feeling the gaze of a few students slide knowingly over her. Well, she said to herself, she had nothing to be secretive about. Honestly. So what if Merlon Tower was an old-school somewhat lecherous nut? She couldn't help that.

Once the classroom was empty, he asked her if she'd like a ride home.

That's okay, she said. I'm not far.

He persisted as they began down the stairs. Had she seen the new park by the river?

What river? she said.

No? he said, throwing up his hands. He was like a conductor when he taught, using his body and sweeping gestures to accentuate his points. She was about to graduate, he said in his gravelly voice, and she had not even seen the river?

Though an undergraduate, Sophie had been allowed into the graduate class on Mr. Tower's special say-so. She had taken his writing workshop the year before, sitting in kidney-shaped desk-and-chair sets, listening to him rant and rave—against the administration, against a culture that didn't appreciate good writing, against the pressure to conform.

Think! Think! he told his students. *Don't accept what is presented to you!*

Question it all!

The messages they have been giving you are wrong!
Take nothing on faith.

He was a published author—essays, articles, even books—
impressive to an undergraduate. Sophie had first signed up for
his class aware he also had a reputation for being *one of those guys*.
He'd written a famous article in a prominent men's magazine
called "Up the Down Coed" in which he highlighted what he saw
as the inevitable dynamic between a red-blooded professor and
his nubile female students. She had not read the essay—in fact,
she didn't know anyone who actually had—but his point apparently was that people shouldn't expect people not to be human!
In a time when females were seizing rights long-oppressed for
the equality they deserved—something which was so obvious to
Sophie she was surprised it needed pointing out—Tower's ren-
egade attitude was outrageous and even radical, in its way.

No, it wasn't his finest hour, but he turned out to be an inspiring teacher—one who didn't care what anyone thought. In fact,
that's what he banged on about. *Be yourself! Your voice is the only
one you've got! No one's going to stick up for your work but you!* So if
Sophie recognized something creepy, she ignored it—that wasn't
the part of R. M. Tower that she experienced.

In class he had roamed the front of the classroom in a tattered
tweed jacket and rumpled unbuttoned shirt, his head like that of
a scarred lion, with jowls and pockmarked skin, a rubbery mouth
and popping eyes and tobacco-stained teeth, ranting against the
"expected ways" and the deadening "educational factory lines." He
sang the praises of the beautiful sentence and the original stylist.

Tell us what *you* see! he bellowed.

He radiated radical sparks in a number of directions—from challenging narrative convention to boycotting faculty meetings for the small percentage of black colleagues. In class, he had been encouraging to Sophie about her writing—stream-of-consciousness stories both playful and melancholy—and at the end of her junior year suggested rather offhandedly that she take his graduate workshop; her work was good enough.

In the graduate class they sat at a long table in a room on an upper floor with a large paned window, like a solarium.

One winter day he'd come into class with a long arrow from a bow under his arm. It wasn't quite a child's arrow, but it wasn't a hardy real arrow either. Tower began talking about Marianne Moore's poem "Poetry" with the famous line of "imaginary gardens with real toads in them."

He lifted the arrow, speaking with mounting enthusiasm of the poetic "bow," representing the imagination, and to demonstrate the realness of the arrow (like the toad?) he snapped the arrowhead off its stem. The class watched as he slid the triangular arrowhead like a shuffleboard disk down the wooden table rather deliberately to where Sophie sat in front of her open notebook. She touched the arrow as if to complete the demonstration that it was indeed real, and left it sitting there. The whole class seemed to wince a little, even as they smiled.

They moved on to the discussion of the story that week, a story about a woman who accidentally kills an old man sleeping under her car, the tragedy of which registered weakly with Sophie. Her state of mind was so steeped in thoughts of loss and death that any depiction of its being remarkable or upsetting were tin in her ear.

Next to her at the table, a long-armed student named Keith Ferris who wrote stories about buffoonish fellows in improbable situations had idly picked up the arrow and throughout the class jiggled it in his shaky fingers, used it as a drumstick, tossed it like a cat playing with a mouse.

When class was over and everyone rose, Mr. Tower barked out from the end of the table. Mr. Ferris! Have you taken the arrow intended for Miss Vincent?

A few leaving students glanced back with interest.

Keith Ferris stammered, Ah, ah . . . no.

Students now looked away, not wanting to witness someone having his knuckles rapped. Sophie saw Keith blush, and felt mortified.

Here, Keith said, not meeting Sophie's eye, and deposited the arrow on top of the notebook she had just closed. She slid notebook and arrow into her black canvas bag.

As she made for the door she noticed Mr. Tower, under the guise of observing the filing out of students, shoot her a bland but meaningful look which she pretended she did not see, and therefore did not have to acknowledge.

•

The May afternoon was bright and cool with a low breeze as she and Merlon Tower walked on the uneven brick sidewalk past brittle lilacs gone brown in their rich green hedges.

A fine green net was thrown over the upper branches of spreading trees; pink petals rolled in the gutters.

Did they walk side by side? Mr. Tower probably carried his unclosed briefcase with papers sticking up, pressed against his open tweed coat, maybe securing with his other arm more sliding books or a bound manuscript with a clear cover.

She didn't remember.

She did remember what she was wearing—a loose sundress to her knee, lilac colored, with cap sleeves and square-necked smocking.

It might have been awkward walking beside Mr. Tower, but she would probably not have felt it so much. Though it had been four months earlier when her mother had died, Sophie was still in shock. On an icy morning in January, her mother had been driving down the avenue where they lived on the winding coast north of Boston on her way to an exercise class. When her car crossed the familiar railroad tracks, it had been struck like a bull's-eye by the train going by. The crossing signals had failed to work, having been frozen in an ice storm the night before. She'd been killed instantly.

Sophie had taken two weeks off from school, staying at home with her six siblings and disoriented father. There'd been a blizzard and a parade of friends and casseroles, sleepless nights and cigarettes and rueful jokes. There were the younger siblings to

worry about. She returned having only four months till graduation, so the idea of stopping before the finish line, so to speak,
was never raised, even if she felt that school now had turned thoroughly meaningless—she had often felt it meaningless, but it
turned out she'd no idea how meaningless something could actually be!—and she floated through her classes in a numb air of
shock. When she'd heard the news on the phone it had torn a
hole in her and she went immediately hard and did not cry. If she
let herself feel, the part of her that was left would be riddled with
holes and there'd be nothing left. She had not, since then, shed a
tear. Her body shut down; to allow feeling would sink her.

So she attended classes which were thoroughly altered now,
as if a water wash had brushed over everything, streaking lines
and pulling the color out.

Grief turned out to be slow moving. Situations which at
another time would be anxious-making were far less so now.
What did anything matter? What could possibly be worrisome?
She would, therefore, have been less nervous than usual to walk
with Mr. Tower to his car.

They might have talked about what she planned to do after
graduation or maybe about her family situation.

When she looked back she could remember little of that
spring, of her classes. She remembered seeing the movie *The
Battle of Algiers* and being shaken by it, the war depicted with such
horror she was able to feel that. She remembered the classes with
Mr. Tower because writing was something she cared about. She
felt, though, suspended, as if she'd stepped off a seaside cliff, but

for some miraculous reason had not plunged down to the rocks and surf, but continued merely to walk in the air over the great drop beneath her.

Eventually they arrived at a small beaten-up car—a Datsun?—tipped on the hill. Sophie paid little attention to cars. Waiting by the passenger door while Mr. Tower unlocked the driver's side, she had looked in the back, surprised by the mess. It was bucket deep in aluminum soda cans, glass bottles, and wrappers, and its back seat was scattered with paperbacks, files, flattened jackets, empty potato-chip bags. Inside, Mr. Tower reached across the front seat and unlocked her door, a gesture for a split second oddly intimate. But so many things were odd then. She was seeing, in fact, that things being weird were far more plentiful than things being normal. She was aware that this revelation now prevented her from being constantly surprised or charmed, as she used to be, by weird and unexpected things. She opened her door. It was quiet inside and smelled of stale smoke and rotten apple cores and cigarette butts.

Though it's just as possible that as they walked to his car, Merlon Tower had talked about some injustice or some thing he was outraged by. And that the car was unlocked, as it could have been in those days.

Sophie remembered getting in and the too-close smell, but she did not remember the drive. The night before, she also remembered, she'd pulled an all-nighter, finishing a paper, it being the last week of school, and she had been feeling that spaciness of no sleep and of sandy eyes when your body feels either a little heavier or a little lighter, depending on how the fatigue is hitting you.

Then somehow they arrived there, in the parking area of a refurbished park. There was a new concrete promenade and a breeze making the newly planted saplings shiver.

An esplanade ran along a river which she had seen as they drove in but could not see now. Mr. Tower reached behind his seat and fished around in all the crap back there. He pulled out a silver flask and unscrewed the top. He took a swig. Did he really just do that? she thought feeling a trapdoor drop inside her. A swig?

She remembered thinking at least she was not wearing anything sexy. It wasn't her leotard or a short skirt with boots. Had she ever worn either to class? God, maybe she had. Then she remembered she'd worn her leotard with her green tiered peasant skirt to their student-teacher conference—as the meetings were weirdly called—when she'd gone to his actual house the one time. And that, now that she thought about it, had frankly been weird. But then it was always peculiar to see a teacher outside the classroom in the real world. Seeing them join the banal world, they would turn more banal in it.

He lived about a half mile from campus. The house was relatively large, painted gray shingles, in the style of the city, on a rise above the sidewalk, with a lawn swelling up from a low stone wall. A cement walkway banked with shrunken snowbanks led to an echoing porch. Sophie had rung the doorbell and gotten no response. Narrow paned windows on either side of the door showed the sheen of a wooden hall inside. Dim natural light came from windows another room away. She knocked then on the black door and waited. After a while a shadow inside darkened the floor sheen.

The heavy door was opened and in front of her stood a teenage girl with an unimpressed expression, light brown hair parted on the side. She was wearing a light blue Fair Isle sweater with the snowflake design around the neck, in contrast to her dead eyes. Sophie said hi, and that she was there to see her father.

The girl swung her head like a horse and stepped back. I'll let him know someone's here, she said, and gestured for her to wait in the room across from them. Gloom in the hall, winter light on a dark green sofa which Sophie approached and sat on. Another figure passed in the hall going the other way, a younger traipsing boy—the son—who didn't glance at her, used to seeing students in the house. Or girls. Sophie felt a wave of creepiness. His "Up the Down Coed" now seemed more condemning, here in his house. Then she immediately dismissed it, rejecting herself as being part of any cliché. And, really, Mr. Tower was like a troll, and old.

Another person's heeled footsteps entered the hall, continuing the feeling that she was an exhibit being viewed by a parade of family members. This time it was the wife clicking by. Was her name Joan? Sophie vaguely knew she was a writer, too, with her own last name. She wore a narrow skirt above heavy calves, and a cardigan sweater, with her hair up in a twist. She paused in the hallway, not stepping toward the arched entryway.

Hello, the wife said, holding a cigarette piquantly at her jaw.

Does he know you're here? Even in the shadow Sophie felt the appraising look.

I think so, she said. Your daughter let me in.

The wife lifted her chin and dropped it conclusively and walked blithely away.

Sophie resisted the urge to get up and leave.

Where was he anyway. And why was he making her wait?

A girl was used to creepiness from men. The leer from the guy at the newsstand, the crude comment from some jerk standing at the bus stop. One felt a prickly buzz in the bloodstream. One learned to ignore it, and to drop it as quickly as possible.

Sophie did admire the girls who were able to spar back to the rude whistle with a snappy line. Showing outrage sometimes made you feel you weren't so vulnerable.

More than feeling danger or finding insult, Sophie was intrigued by the fact that simply by being female, regardless of personality or size or even age, you were a target for the random shot of—she wasn't sure what to call it—male aggression? Expression? Joy? Scorn?

Sometimes she could see an expression of desire, crass as it was, and that was intriguing. She'd learned early on that desire contained some of life's more magical and fascinating aspects. And she had experienced desire enough to know that the transports of sex were pleasures of the highest inexplicable order. So it was eerily breathtaking when men showed boldness in this department. Of course, her body did not register the boldness that way. At the first sign of any affront, her body would register it as danger—not intrigue or wonder—and its defenses would kick in.

Bottom line, she learned that a girl alone should be on guard. What was he doing in there?

She sat in the winter dusk on his stupid couch. Finally he appeared in the doorway, ragged-headed, looking shorter. She'd only seen him in the classroom, up close.

Miss Vincent, he said. There you are, he added as if he'd been the one waiting. Come along this way then.

Carrying her coat and canvas bag, she followed him through more darkness down the hall to a study walled with bookshelves and with a block of a desk behind which Mr. Tower seated himself. A bay window faced out on the front lawn farther down from where she'd come in, and an occasional car hummed by on the white salted road. She had walked there on a sidewalk pocked with holes cut out of dirty ice sharp as crème brûlée.

Years later she would not remember what they talked about, though she remembered—she *thought*—the configuration of him in his place behind the desk and her in a chair in front. They would most likely have discussed the story she'd submitted, and certainly the death of her mother, only a few weeks previous. She'd missed some of his classes. She was able to describe and talk about her mother's death without crying, though she had picked up a peculiar sort of stutter. She did not feel herself in the world on the surface of things where life was happening. Her emotions had taken the form of a huge churning ball of adrenaline circulating through her, with her real self strangely still and hard at its center. The emotions waiting to accost her swirled outside the thick skin of her refusal to respond to this as a normal person would, to fall apart and to weep, to grieve whether it was listlessly or voluptuously. No, this was too big to respond to in any expected way. It was too big to respond to at all.

The stories she'd been writing around that time were post-modern experiments, with characters struggling with dark fragmentary thoughts and longing and the surprised recognition of the absurdity of time.

This also not remembered.

As for that day of visiting Mr. Tower where he lived, she remembered the house being underlit and wearing her green peasant skirt, being eyed by each member of the family, given a particularly cool appraisal by the wife, and how she was made to wait. She remembered nothing said, no words.

•

So there they were now, parked. There they were, always. Mr. Tower had just taken a swig from the silver flask. A lens seemed to alter the scene and a Novocain feeling coated the air.

Then, as if there were any doubt as to the lurid turn this excursion had taken, he looked at her sideways, with an actual leer, and said, in his croaking voice, Let's speak in a language any cat or dog could understand.

The words drained the car cabin of what little oxygen was left.

She did not respond. Or maybe she mumbled non-words.

Later when she thought back on it, she saw how the overture could not have been less conducive to a response. It wasn't even a question. What was he talking about? That is, she knew precisely what he was talking about—her body alarm was alerted—but what did he actually expect that she do? It was such a demented thing to say; she couldn't imagine what response he might have hoped for. That she bark? Laugh? That she jump on him? It was ridiculous.

Yet, it also was terrifying.

She also thought, Really? Me?
The effort is toward me? That was hard to compute.

No physical contact had been made yet her body felt hit with the same force as if she'd been thrown to the ground. Her nerves vibrated with adrenaline, numbing her.

The language of cats and dogs indeed. Her animal instinct said, Freeze. In the back of her mind was another flag waving . . . Flee! But instinct, faster than reason, knew this was less feasible. To open the door and run would somehow make it worse, more dramatic. To bolt and go running down the waterway . . . she was not even sure where exactly she was, or how far they had come. No, wait it out, said her hammering heart.

He wouldn't do anything more.

It wasn't as if a gun had been pulled on her or anything, so why did she have the feeling of fearing for her life? The highway close call or the stumble at the top of stairs spikes an adrenaline shot of fear, which immediately vanishes when your car swerves in time or the banister is grabbed. But the jolt of fear now bloomed like a cloud of black ink, filling the car with danger.

Also, she felt embarrassed. Also, she felt ashamed, the shame one feels at not having done a sufficient job of looking after the one person you're supposed to keep track of: yourself.

Also, it was such an odd thing to say, not his usual way of speaking. She thought for a split second she was hallucinating. Maybe it was the all-nighter hitting her.

Later she would learn that a mistrust of one's senses was a normal reaction to situations like this. Though the body is alerted and absolutely certain about what is happening, the brain might try to find a way to reason out of it. Was there a word for disbelief in one's own senses?

That Tower was making a pass at her was baffling enough. She was genuinely surprised. Was there a compliment in it somewhere? Her body did not think so: an electric buzz had shot through her and her tired heart was throbbing.

She had sometimes tried to take the attitude she saw practiced by other girls—of arrogance and dismissal, of seeming not to care, and was relieved in the rare times when a man's approach did in fact leave her neutral if not cold. But those times were rare.

When a man made a move toward you, it could have a hypnotic effect. A strange chemistry happened. The appraising look—down to the feet, then back up to the face—could not be ignored. One's blood fizzed regardless—on guard, repelled, and maybe even flattered.

She did not register it then, but thought later how different this was electrically from her usual thrilled reaction to the boy she liked, Curtis, of the long black eyelashes, who sometimes gave her velvety looks and leaned on a radiator lingering while they discussed their admiration for Beckett. But Curtis's attentions were intermittent. He had a girlfriend—she was still in high school, a quiet beauty from a prominent family, famous for having posed in a "High School Playmate" spread in *Playboy*.

So she stared ahead. Concrete pathways. Acid-green leaves on trembling saplings.

The esplanade to the right where not many people were had a railing of gray aluminum. A man walking by adjusted his baseball cap in the wind as if resetting a compass. A woman jogged along with a high swinging ponytail, the soles of her sneakers representing the normal world and the peace and safety there.

Maybe she made that up, the woman running. Still, it reflected the truth of her feeling.

After your mother dies suddenly, you're no longer as taken aback by surprises as you might have been before. You learn the truth that terrible things happen *out of the blue*—a breezy phrase her mother liked to use. You feel then as if there will be no blow equal to that terrible blow, and you may be right. In a life of receiving blows, there must be, after all, one blow with the strongest impact.

It was hard to measure now if Mr. Tower's suggestion to speak in a language any cat or dog could understand would have been more shocking if her mother had not been dead, or to know if indeed he would have chosen to venture such a proposal to her were her mother still alive.

Did he think such an idiotic thing would actually work?

It was the same impulse behind the street catcalls, behind the swagger lines thrown from a pack of boys, or the murmured innuendo of a man maybe not even wanting to be heard—as if the men were tossing things extravagantly overboard, gestures to demonstrate how far their throws could go, or how little they cared for the tossed object.

Few of those things did Sophie consider at the time.

She was simply there: frozen in the fish tank of his littered car, an image which remained intact for forty years.

And for those next forty years every time Sophie thought of that moment, it would be the same clip that played. Only when she thought longer about it did she uncover parts which had been there all along. It was as if a fog blew off the scenes nearby, revealing them, and her attention brought other moments back to her. Think of all the moments that remain unrecovered, she marveled now, and how strange that a new experience can come from only revisiting an unremembered thing. Nothing new happens, yet if our mind looks again, it can find a new experience in something old. In this way, rumination turns out to be an experience after all, revealing to us new layers in our past.

He must have driven her home.

She couldn't remember though. She remembered nothing after the swig from the flask and what he said.

Or probably not all the way home. She would have asked to be let out as soon as the streets looked familiar. They would have gotten close to the college's Main Street with the bookstores and corner bars and House of Pancakes and spider-plant sandwich places and banks. She would have gotten out of the car as soon as possible.

The next memory she had was of either that afternoon or maybe the next day being in the kitchen in the house she rented with some of her other housemates, with its wide wooden floor, and of the airy feeling of classes being over and of spring and people starting to pack, and of telling the story to whoever happened to be in there, getting tea or smoking butts. Her friend Alison was there. Alison had been in her class with Mr. Tower the year before and had come over to discuss what happened. Alison was saying Sophie had to do something. One of her housemates, Tom, a gangly guy who kept track of the telephone and electric bills, said that she should report Tower. No one else agreed this would be effective. It would only involve Sophie more, and it was not, as another housemate, Melanie, said, twisting at her dreadlocks, in any way cool. How the hell could the administration help?

Alison suggested Sophie write Tower an angry letter. Sophie repeated she really didn't want to have anything more to do with him. Alison reminded her of the arrow incident, and Sophie told everyone that story and people laughed—it was the first time she made people laugh with the story, as she would continue to do over the next forty years—and Sophie admitted she still had the stupid arrow. She didn't know why she'd kept it, because it had been so embarrassing, but perhaps that was why. Tom wondered what was Sophie taking a class with Tower anyway when she knew the guy was a sleaze and Alison rolled her eyes, indicating he had no idea what he was talking about. Melanie explained, Because if that was a consideration you wouldn't take half of the classes taught by guys.

That's interesting, said another housemate, Mark, who had majored in linguistics, because traditionally an arrow is a symbol of protection. He was bobbing a tea bag in a mug of steaming water.

Right, said Melanie. Except when it's violence?

The general consensus then was that Sophie should return the arrow. She could leave it in Tower's faculty box and not have to see him. It was something, at least.

So a few days later, on the weekend when teachers were scarce, Sophie took the snapped-off arrow to Watson House, a maroon sandstone building with a depressed archway, which housed the English department. She walked stealthily down an empty hall to the wooden grid of cubbyholes, each labeled with a faculty member's name. Instead of placing the arrow down in the cubby, she stuck its point into the wooden side. It looked as if a sprite might have launched it there from some magical forest—a make-believe forest, no doubt—and she had a small satisfaction at how out of place it looked there.

Two days later she got a letter in her own PO box with her address typed, and inside on small white stationery with *R. M. Tower* engraved at the top, the following message, also typed:

> *Dear Sophie,*
> *At least your spoiled stricken frigid little hand had enough gumption to spear the arrow into my box. Perhaps a good sign. I hope that one day you may forgive your parents for having failed you.*
>
> *Sincerely,*

. . . and the scrawl indicating his name.

•

Her family would be arriving the morning of graduation, and the night before, her last night at college, Sophie went to a string of blowout parties dotted across campus. At some point she ended up randomly paired with a pale boy who was a friend of a friend of the boy she liked, Curtis. The pale boy went to another college and was not someone she was particularly attracted to, but he focused on her on the dance floor at one of the last parties and surprised her by twirling her around like a lassoing cowboy, making her laugh inside with embarrassment. They ended up crashing on the floor of an empty apartment with a dozen other people also crashing around them. Drunkenly at 3:00 a.m. in the dark and among the quiet strangers, the pale boy kissed her. She was not repelled, but not compelled either. She felt it blankly. He untied the halter string at her neck.

"You have nice breasts," he said in a formal way. After not too long she let him push aside the flounces of her peasant skirt and pull off her underpants and try to enter her. Her body was unreceptive. She felt the nerves in him fluttering and tried to channel some of that energy since he was so close, but they did not know each other and their bodies did not understand each other. She was dry and felt blocked. It's not going to work, she thought, tired and loosely drunk, but he persevered and kept pushing and he got halfway in and she helped him to all the way. The magic transport she was so enchanted by stirred in her hips and she felt a swoon distantly, but it did not seem as real, or as important as it usually was. Trying to keep his breath quiet, the pale boy sounded as if he was gasping in frozen air. It crossed her mind they might be heard, but all the bodies around them were oddly still, sleeping or passed out.

She lay there as a deep blue light appeared in the windows, and thought how she was more sophisticated now having had sex which was not important to her. After dozing awhile she sat up, shook the boy's shoulder, and said goodbye. She walked home in the shadowless dawn and felt the vast mystery, as one did in the dawn light. She thought how usually you just slept through it, this most magic moment of the day, and how it was perhaps like our existence, little noticing the vast mystery. She marveled too how dawn was also, in fact, something which happened monotonously by rote without interruption every twenty-four hours—

hardly unusual—and had done so for thousands, if not millions, of years.

The next morning her family was there.

Three of Sophie's six siblings had made it, with her father and her aunt, all driving the two hours from home. With them, she wove through the vast plots of gray metal foldout chairs to find them seats out of the unrelenting sun. She steered them to the back since Aunt Mimi, her mother's sister, preferred shade, despite wearing a navy brimmed hat, a perfect match to her navy Chanel suit with the white piped lapel and pockets. Her father wore his eternal gray work suit with its short pants and incessantly jiggled change in his pocket as he gazed over the heads of his children with an expression that said it did not expect to find anything of interest in the distance either. Everyone felt the austerity of the occasion in the heavy absence of Mum, who had been a particular appreciator of ceremonies. She would dress up in something cheerful and stylish and have her hair done and bring presents for not just her child being celebrated, but for a few of the child's friends, too. Minnie, now eight, was her uncomplaining soldier-self in short pigtails, having conceded to wearing a dress, but being allowed, something their mother would not have, to wear sneakers. Chase, at thirteen, had dressed up in a blue-and-white-striped button-down shirt, one shirttail tucked in, one flapping out. The hair in his eyes was long, perhaps in need of a haircut.

Her sister Caitlin, her thick hair looped in a part with two barrettes, wore a cream-colored dress with shoulder pads. Caitlin made a show of glaring fiercely when Sophie pointed out R. M. Tower sitting with the other eminent English faculty members on the makeshift stage in front of Watson Hall where the English majors were to receive their diplomas.

The graduates sat in the front rows, dressed in the black full-armed robes. Sophie had a red band around one upper arm to indicate her protest of the university's investments in South Africa and its apartheid rule. Underneath she wore her lilac dress. The graduates' black board hats were like dull sequins making a hovering mosaic. Sophie had her usual feeling in a crowd, of everyone somehow belonging there but herself. She found her alphabetical spot with her class near the back.

Sitting waiting to be called, Sophie felt the buzz of lack of sleep, once again having been up all night, and not yet the need, which could strike anytime, of the desire to nod off. She also felt the pleasant blur of after-sex, that thing you could never feel on your own. It was something you got only after physically communing with another body. The blurred state was something she could value as something only hers, private, despite its not being particularly meaningful, but it had been a version of connecting to something more than only herself.

Her row of chairs stood and turned to the right. Filing into a line snaking up to the stage, they advanced toward the steps. She glanced back to where her family sat and saw Aunt Mimi's blue-and-white hat and Caitlin's white dress. Where was Dad? Probably deeper in the shadows, having removed himself to smoke.

At the far end of the platform the dean, a woman with springy gray hair and a receding chin, was announcing the graduates' names into a microphone. Then it was her turn—the dean said her name, *Sophie Paine Vincent.* Sophie stepped up and moved across the stage, feeling the eyes of her family on her like pallbearers. Her red band of protest was on the stage side and she regretted it didn't show. At the time, she believed she would continue, after graduation, to protest and fiercely fight and defend the rights of living things, humans and animals both. First she had planned to spend the summer driving the perimeter of the country. Other friends were headed to Europe, but she felt she should see her own country first. Alone, she would end up driving for a month clockwise from New England, down through the South, up the western coast and back along through all the northern states, ending up at Niagara Falls, sleeping in the back of the car and writing in a journal, beginning the first direct acquaintance with being alone out in the world for an extended period of time which ended up being a kind of arrow indicating the career she would eventually make for herself, as a writer.

She crossed the stage and shook hands with Mr. Weinstock who had taught her a truly inspiring class on Proust, then shook hands with Ms. Havercloss, the feminist with her feather earrings whom she'd never studied with, and, when she came to R. M. Tower, in his robe with a green-and-yellow capelet over the shoulders, she walked purposefully by, refusing to look at him, even if it made her feel weirdly disoriented. After getting her diploma, one of the last on the table, she descended the stairs and moved the tassel dangling off her square hat from the right side to the left. In the distance despite the massive crowd she could pick out Caitlin's face and her reliable knowing smile.

.   .   .

Forty years later she still remembered being in the car and the language of cats and dogs. She remembered the lilac dress and the flask, remembered the arrow and the note and refusing the offered hand.

Afterward, whenever she was alone with a man, particularly one older, she would feel the usual animal trepidation. For the rest of her life, in fact, pretty much every time she was one-on-one with a man, she would find herself wary and untrusting and on guard.

But that was simply how things were. After all, the truth of it was, if he wanted to, a man could snap her arm in half.

Acknowledgments

Warmest thanks to Georges and Anne Bonchandt for their decades of devoted service.

Thanks to my early readers, cherished friends, Lucy Winton, Jackie Sohier, Sarah Paley, Sara Goodman, Sasha Wade, Hope Pingree, Nancy Lemann, Tamara Weiss, Dorothy Gallagher; thanks to my students who teach me, noting core members Jimmy Jung, Cat Greenman, Chloe Malle; thanks to beloved sisters Carrie, Eliza, and Dinah for extra reinforcements.

Thanks for further help from Jean and Gordon Douglas, Jay Anania, Jean Pagliuso, Caio Fonseca, brothers George and Chris, Lily Thorne, Mott Hupfel, Carolyn Roumeguère, Brian Sawyer, Francesca Marciano, Caroline Kennedy, Al Styron, Elizabeth Kling, Jonathan Ames, Huger Foote, Elvis Perkins, Lorrie Moore, Amy Hempel, Evan Young, George Bell, ex-husbands Charlie and Davis, and Pingrees Hannah, Cecily, and Asa.

Thanks to the cracker team at Knopf, amazing in a time of amazement.

Thanks to daughter, Ava, who helped type some of these babies into the twenty-first century; and not least thanks to my incomparable editor, Jordan Pavlin, to whom this book is with love dedicated.

A NOTE ABOUT THE AUTHOR

Susan Minot is an award-winning novelist, short-story
writer, poet, screenwriter, and playwright. Her first novel,
Monkeys, was published in a dozen countries and won the
Prix Femina Étranger in France. Her novel *Evening* was a
worldwide best seller and became a major motion picture.
She lives in New York City where she teaches writing and
on North Haven Island in Maine.

A NOTE ON THE TYPE

This book was set in Scala, a typeface designed by the Dutch designer Martin Majoor (b. 1960) in 1988 and released by the FontFont foundry in 1990. While designed as a fully modern family of fonts containing both a serif and a sans serif alphabet, Scala retains many refinements normally associated with traditional fonts.

Typeset by Scribe,
Philadelphia, Pennsylvania
Printed and bound by Berryville Graphics,
Berryville, Virginia
Designed by Soonyoung Kwon